FREE FALL TO BLACK

JOHN H. CUNNINGHAM

Other books by John H. Cunningham

Red Right Return
Green to Go
Crystal Blue
Second Chance Gold
Maroon Rising

FREE FALL TO BLACK

JOHN H. CUNNINGHAM

FREE FALL TO BLACK

Copyright © 2017 John H. Cunningham

All rights reserved. No part of this book may be reproduced or retransmitted in any form or by any means without the written permission of the publisher.

Published by Greene Street, LLC

Print ISBN: 978-0-9987965-0-5
Electronic ISBN: 978-0-9987965-1-2

The events and characters in this book are fictitious. Certain real locations and public figures are mentioned, but have been used fictitiously, and all other characters and events in the book have been invented.

www.jhcunningham.com

Acknowledgements

Free Fall to Black has been a long time coming. It's been a hectic year since Maroon Rising was released, and the restoration of my house in Key West has prolonged the process, but is already the source of many new inspirations. Thank you for your patience.

It's always fascinating how authors weave aspects of their own lives into their fiction, and I'm certainly no different. Whether characters, places, names, friends, incidents, history, observations or subliminal suggestions from day-to-day life, there are many of these threads woven into the series. Friends, and fans of the Buck Reilly series may recognize a few things herein, or even from my social media sites, but trust me when I say that Free Fall to Black is full of these elements. See if you can spot any…

As with the past several books, I've also combined music into the story, and would like to thank Dave McKenney for co-writing and recording Long View Off a Short Pier (and Blues to Brown) on his cd Back in Time, and also for appearing in this book. Thanks also to Keith Sykes for agreeing to appear, and for continuing to co-write a song which we have yet to complete, but hope to soon. It's a beauty. I believe that combining music into the Buck Reilly adventures adds another dimension to help you to enjoy the ride. I hope you agree.

Thanks also to my friend and publicist, Ann-Marie Nieves of Get Red PR, for her unwavering support, brainstorming, energy, introductions and creativity. You're the best. Also to

Tim Harkness for creating the book cover, illustrations, logos and advertisements. Thanks also to Steve Troha at Folio Literary Management and Dana Spector at Paradigm Agency.

Thank you to the team at The Editorial Department (TED): Renni Browne, Ross Browne, and Shannon Roberts. I've worked with TED as my editorial team for 20 years, and they do an amazing job.

And finally, to my lovely ladies Holly, Bailey and Cortney, thank you for your love and support. Never give up on your dreams, some day they may actually come true…

"The two hardest things in life to handle are success and failure."
African proverb

*This book is for my Key West gang:
Carl, Shawn, Patrick, Mike, Deb, Sam, and Noel.
…The Rum Bunch…*

Contents

SECTION 1 A KING IS CROWNED 15

SECTION 2 LEARN FROM THE WRONG THINGS YOU'VE DONE 73

SECTION 3 LIFE IN THE FAST LANE 119

SECTION 4 WHEN THE WHIP COMES DOWN 171

SECTION 5 WHEN THE MUSIC'S OVER, TURN OUT THE LIGHTS 239

SECTION 1

A KING IS CROWNED

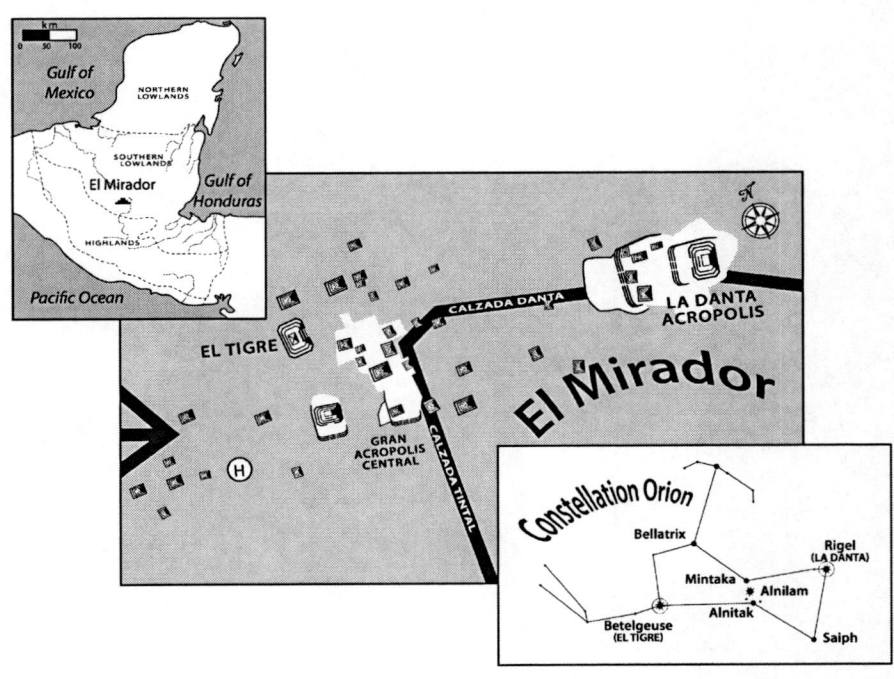

1

2006

What had once been a city of more than a hundred thousand people was now a jungle wasteland. From the peak of the La Danta pyramid, 230 feet above the stony ground below, the air felt thin, the sun burned my exposed skin, and the view of flat green canopy was endless.

"Hard to believe we're on top of the largest pyramid in the world," the voice next to me said.

Scarlet Roberson, my associate at e-Antiquity, looked out over El Mirador. The former Mayan city had been larger than modern Los Angeles.

"Buck?" she said.

"Where'd they go, Red?"

She leaned over the edge of the flat stone surface and peered down toward our base camp.

"Everyone's still here—"

"Two thousand years ago, El Mirador was the center of the Mayan world, and then—poof, gone." My voice sounded faint in the breeze. "What happened?"

Scarlet stood with her hands on her hips. "We're not here for the Mayan people, we're here for their missing treasury."

I turned to face her. The dimple in her right cheek was pinched. Her green eyes were squinted—the sun was behind me—and her red ponytail fluttered in the breeze.

"Right," I said. "And we'll have to think like they did to figure out where they stored their riches."

"You bring a Ouija board? Tarot cards? Divining rod?"

I squeezed her arm. "I don't need any of that."

"I hope you're right, Buck. You know the cost of this expedition is freaking Jack out more than any one we've ever done."

"That's because our CEO's become more of a glorified bean counter than ever," I said. "Doesn't matter, he'll be happy. El Mirador has the potential to be the greatest find in history."

"We've been here for a month. The news people are getting antsy. Predicting success with all that certainty may have been a little too bold."

"I'm feeling bold. I'm feeling like a conqueror, dammit. And the way e-Antiquity's stock has been kicking ass, when I…when *we* pull this off, we'll be the talk of every newspaper in the world."

Her gaze panned over the many stone structures below us and stopped on the opposite side of the clearing where our large safari tents were pitched.

"The ministry officials won't keep one of their top archeological sites closed for much longer—even for us," she said.

"I can feel it, Scarlet. Trust me, okay?"

She nodded slowly, staring up into my eyes.

We stood there another ten minutes studying details of the heavily eroded city center. Many other buildings, from temples to storehouse foundations, peeked out from the thick green vegetation. I was very familiar with the overall site plan and each of the known buildings, but from this height I could also see El Mirador's multiple triadic structures. Historians had concluded that the cluster of three buildings—which typically included one main building flanked on each side by a smaller one—formed triangles in homage to the constellation Orion, which the Mayans considered the seat of creation. I shook my head, baffled—as astronomers had been for centuries. How the hell had the Mayans pulled this off? Especially since the Europeans hadn't discovered the Orion nebula until 1611.

In the distance I could see remnants of other pre-classical Mayan cities—together with El Mirador they created an even larger triadic configuration. The shape being central to the Mayan DNA, the treasury had to be in a location related to these triadic structures.

I said, "Let's go review the documents again."

Going down a pyramid is always more difficult than going up, and my boots scraped loose gravel and moss that tumbled down below me. The sight of pebbles spinning through the air and bouncing off rock steps didn't stop my brain from working to decode the mystery of the Mayan treasury, any more than did my awareness that most scholars considered it a myth. The Mayans were not known to have worshipped golden idols, precious jewels, or silver. But they'd built a vast empire with hundreds of thousands of citizens and dominated the region for thousands of years across what today are Mexico, Belize, Guatemala, and Honduras. My gut told me they didn't do all that on sheer will alone, and rulers as powerful as the most noteworthy here at El Mirador, Reino Kan and his heirs, had surely amassed tremendous fortunes in the process. Hell, that was just human nature.

And while the Mayans were many things, they were still men and women when it came right down to it. That, and their being as greedy as people are today, is what I was banking on, and according to Jack Dodson, my co-founder and partner at e-Antiquity, our company had bet the farm on it.

2

"You know how important this is, Buck." Jack Dodson's voice crackled over the speaker of my satellite phone. "And while your *gut* is certain about the existence of the Mayan treasury, the market's very nervous. If we have to raise more equity it'll reduce the value of our stock, which means our investors will shit bricks."

"Remember the tenth grade, Jack?"

"What are you talking about?"

"When we created the largest volcano in the history of the DC area for our science project, and the school wanted to shut us down?"

A brief chuckle tickled my ear. "With the scuba tank, road flares, and liquid asphalt they thought would blow up the gymnasium? Yeah, I remember."

"When Principal Smoller threatened to expel us if we detonated Mount Vesuvius, you called the local TV station and they rushed out to cover our *Guinness Book of World Records* event."

"They actually thought it was really a world record—"

"They thought it was, because you were so convincing," I said. "You'll keep the investors calm, Jack. You always do."

"Just figure it out before I run out of bullshit," he said.

"You? That's not possible, buddy. You're so full of shit the blue eyes you were born with turned brown."

With that I turned the phone off.

I glanced around the inside of the safari tent I'd dragged all over the globe. So many locations, so many calls to provide Jack with ammo to reassure investors that all would be fine. Its wood floor shined with the luster of an Aspen boutique hotel. I smiled in appreciation of the global team comprising my handpicked men, taking care of every detail without reminders. For which they were handsomely paid.

It wasn't yet dusk. The canvas walls were still rolled up, and the gentle breeze wafting the canvas ceiling made it sound like a luffing sail in light wind. My king-size bed was made with blankets folded neatly on the end, ready to grab if the night air had a chill or I was without companionship.

Scarlet walked up the steps into the tent, having showered and changed into shorts and a sleeveless top that accentuated her curves. She held up a bottle of Zacapa Centenario rum in one hand and a sheaf of papers in the other. She plopped into one of the two campaign chairs and leaned over the table where the many maps, documents, notes, and photographs of antiquities were laid out.

After leaving her papers on the bed she took ice from the bucket and dropped it in a crystal glass, then poured amber liquid over it from the nearly full bottle. Behind her on a closed canvas flap was a map for El Mirador and all its buildings—at least those that had been surveyed so far. Triangular shapes jumped out from multiple locations, and their symmetry nagged at me.

"Buck, the men surveyed another section of the northeast region this afternoon." She pointed to the folder on the bed. I knew that inside would be hand-drawn maps showing distances and identifying buildings by exact shape and measurements.

"They didn't find anything."

I puffed out a long breath as the cook brought in a tray of food.

"You two need to eat before it's gone." The sixty-something chef had traveled with me the better part of two years. His long gray beard and shaggy gray hair, parted down the middle the way John Travolta wore his in the 1970s, framed a face with red cheeks and brown eyes that had been known to twinkle.

"Thanks, Cookie," I said.

He spun on his heel and glared at me. He shoved his open hand forward.

"Name's Stu, Stu Berry, pleased to be of service."

"I'm afraid if I call you Stu, you'll think it's a request."

"Very funny. Just stick the tray outside and I'll pick it up so that damn jaguar doesn't come sniffing around again."

As if on cue, we heard a distant roar.

"Too late, Cookie. He's already smelled your chow."

White teeth flashed a big smile from the bush of gray beard.

"I'll load my rifle. A jaguar head will be the perfect addition to my den back in Utah."

With that he was gone, and soon after so was the food he'd brought us. Scarlet refilled my glass and undid another button on her shirt front.

"I'd better review what the men found today," I said. I meant it, though I was feeling a bit hazy and Scarlet was now sitting next to me on the bed.

The new surveys were of a thousand-foot section in the northeastern edge of the city. There were two additional triadic groupings, with apparent paths or roads noted and foundations labeled as dwellings. Darkness came, and I realized the men had lowered the rest of the canvas flaps and buttoned down my tent while we were eating. We'd been too focused to notice. Candles and propane lights now flickered.

I reached to pour more rum and was surprised to find the bottle nearly empty. It wasn't just the candlelight causing a haze.

More buttons had somehow come undone on Scarlet's top.

"Not tonight," I said. "I need to focus."

Her fingers were fiddling with my shirt buttons.

I took her hand. "No, Scarlet."

She sat back. "That's not what you said last night. Or in Porto Bello, Cartagena, Morocco—"

"I'm not looking for a relationship, you know that."

"It's okay." She glanced to the mirror and we both caught her reflection. "Whatever happens in the jungle stays in the jungle."

"I need to keep focused. Maybe someday things'll be different."

She finished undoing my shirt buttons—now I was lying flat. When she lay down hard next to me, the sound of paper crumpling made me turn my head, then slide my arm along the bed to push the papers, the engineering surveys, and the documents onto the floor where they landed with a thud.

Her hand was on my chest, her breath hot on my neck. Semi-comatose in a rum fog, I was still aware of my shirt slipping off, followed by my pants, and then her hot body pressed against mine. I rose to the occasion, and we rolled around clumsily until we were spooning.

The heat of the jungle night felt cool compared to the cauldron brewing between our bodies, and even as I was lost unto her, a small voice inside my head kept whispering: "You'll never figure El Mirador out."

3

T<small>HE SUN BEAT THROUGH THE PLASTIC WINDOW AND CUT</small> across my face like scalding water. My eyelids pressed tight as I rolled away and pulled my numb arm from under Scarlet. Her creamy skin glowed, her red hair ablaze against the white sheet. I could hear jungle sounds through the canvas walls, plus the voices of men talking and the scrape of metal as a cart was dropped onto a tow hitch. The air was aromatic with burning wood and cooking food. We'd slept in, and my head ached, but worse, my mouth was dry as dirt. I smacked my lips prospecting for saliva.

The research materials for our expedition were strewn across the floor. I could see the new survey from yesterday atop a detailed map of the area around El Tigre, the second largest pyramid on the site. The drawings and maps were at odd angles, adding to the chaos—

I raised up on my elbow. Chaos *theory*?

A different approach. Chaos theory used random systems to detect small differences suggesting slight anomalies in what were considered predictable outcomes. When problems seemed unsolvable, or the obvious equations didn't add up, chaos theory occasionally provided and effective method of breaking challenges.

Should we reconsider all the fixed dynamics we'd studied for months? The idea of thinking outside the box, inspired by the scattered papers on the floor, now had me licking my cracked lips.

My gaze rose to the site map attached to the canvas wall, followed its contours, and hesitated on each shape. El Tigre pyramid was at the far western edge, cockeyed on its latitude and facing southeast toward the La Danta pyramid on the far eastern edge. The two pyramids—the central structures of El Mirador—were connected by a straight line, the *Calzada* Danta, or Danta Road to us non-Spanish speakers. Other archeologists had concluded that the straight line between the two pyramids was based on the one at a similar angle between two of the main stars in the Orion constellation. I reached down and rooted through the papers for my star map of Orion, having studied it many times for clues.

Popular thought held that the builders had sited La Danta in El Mirador's configuration to a location that corresponded to the star Betelgeuse in Orion. The largest star in the constellation, Betelgeuse was some thousand times greater than our sun. From La Danta, my eyes followed an imaginary line, like the one in Orion's Belt, toward the equivalent location of Alnitak, a medium-sized star on the left side of the constellation, and all the way to the El Tigre pyramid. But as I studied the constellation map and compared it with the aerial shot of the El Mirador, my breath caught. The line was at a slightly different angle from that of Orion's Belt.

I sat up and swung my feet over the side of the bed, my mind moving faster than the blur of hangover could restrain.

Chaos theory.

"Buck?" Scarlet's voice was raspy. "What're you doing?"

"If the Danta Road led to the ruins of Guacamaya, which is situated on the same angle as the one between Betelgeuse and Alnitak," I said, "then La Danta pyramid may actually equate instead to the bottom right star in the constellation, which is the star Rigel."

"What are you talking about?"

I jumped out of bed naked, yanked down on the rope on a side flap of the tent to roll it up, and wrapped the rope around a hook.

"You don't have any clothes on!"

I could hardly keep still. "That would mean that all the previous thinking about El Mirador and Orion has been wrong!"

Scarlet sat up with the sheet covering her breasts.

"What're you saying?"

I bent over the bed. "What's considered the center of the constellation Orion?"

"The middle star in the Belt."

I glanced at the star map. "Alnilam. The brightest star in the constellation—two hundred and fifty thousand times brighter than the sun—"

"Hey, d'you mind lowering the flap?"

"Nice ass, Buck!" Cookie was outside, pointing at me, and the crew, gathered for breakfast, were all laughing. When I yanked the rope again the canvas wall dropped.

"So what's the point?" Scarlet said.

I bent down and grabbed the aerial map of El Mirador.

"If we misconstrued the Danta Road as matching the location of the bottom line of the constellation, and the imaginary line's actually south of that, between El Tigre and Guacamaya, and the Danta pyramid is really Rigel—which makes sense, since Rigel and Betelgeuse are the two largest stars, and they match the two largest structures here—then Alnilam is actually further north."

"But..." Her eyes had grown wide. "That would change everything."

"My point!" I showed her the aerial map and dragged my finger from the point we'd thought corresponded to the center of the constellation in relation to the city, then up to an area of dense green foliage which, if my new theory was correct, would have been the approximate location corresponding to the actual center of the constellation.

Rummaging through the papers, I found the previous day's survey. I extrapolated a couple of locations on the survey and aerial, then ran my finger to a spot between two triadic formations that would correspond to the approximate center of the constellation.

"Right here."

"There's nothing on the survey but jungle—"

"Exactly! Now get some clothes on and let's go check it out!"

4

It had taken four hours to load the gear and crew, get to the closest point on the road to what I was now referring to as the Alnilam site, and hack through the jungle toward the area between the two unnamed triadic structures.

"Cody, I want you to find me this point right here." I pointed on the aerial photograph to where I'd overlain the constellation Orion.

We'd recruited Cody Summers, my lead engineer for the past three years, out of Virginia Tech for his brilliance and his exuberant desire to find treasure, as opposed to designing sanitary lines for housing developments. He gave me a look. Short, plump, and constantly drenched with sweat, he was never deterred yet often wanted to challenge my hypotheses. That look meant one of those moments was coming.

"But—"

"This may be contrary to everything else we've done so far, but I had an epiphany this morning."

He glanced at Scarlet, then back at me. "You mean when you were hopping around naked?"

"Sometimes inspiration hits at inopportune times."

He risked another glance at Scarlet. "I'll say."

With no further debate Cody instructed the men to set up their tripod-based, motorized, robotic, total stations and surveying tools, all connected to a laptop he carried in his backpack.

Scarlet and I watched from the tailgate of our Land Rover while the men used the sophisticated surveying equipment to triangulate their way toward the Alnilam end point.

"I hope you're right about this, Buck."

"I can feel it in my gut." I watched the men, anxious to get digging.

Scarlet nudged me. "Have you noticed those guys?"

Our small press corps had turned out in full. Three journalists, one from the *New York Times*, one from *National Geographic,* and one from *Nuestra Diario*, the most widely circulated newspaper in Central America. The guy from the *Times* also had a photographer. Collectively, they looked more excited than we'd seen them since their arrival weeks ago.

"Piranhas. They smell blood."

"Which is good," she said. "It wasn't easy to convince the *Times* and *National Geographic* to join us here."

I turned to look into Scarlet's eyes.

"Rhodes Scholar, Oxford-trained archeologist, *and* public relations guru. You're a real prize, Red."

When she turned away I realized she might have preferred something more personal, but now wasn't the time. We were on a fresh thread, and it felt to me like it was about to pull all the loose ones tight.

Cody took off his VT hat to wipe his forehead. "Okay, y'all, we have an intersection of points that marks your spot. We staked it."

"Machetes and shovels," I said.

Scarlet shrugged. "The press was hoping for something more out of *Raiders of the Lost Ark*."

I jumped off the Rover's tailgate. "If it were just hidden in some cave it would've been discovered long ago." I smiled. "Let's go make history."

5

THE SPOT CODY HAD IDENTIFIED WAS DEEP IN THICK JUNGLE. Our local team of men whipped their machetes to make quick progress through the surrounding scrub, undergrowth, and saplings until they'd cleared a circular site approximately fifty feet across. With that done, they raked the clearing down to dirt to uncover a small stone pyramid, one foot square and three feet from the stake the survey team had placed in the center of the Alnilam site.

A murmur of excitement passed through the group. The journalists took notes, and the *Times* photographer snapped a couple of pictures.

"Pressure's on, Buck," Scarlet said. "Good luck."

I grabbed a shovel out of the trailer.

"Luck is for the lottery," I said.

I stood for a moment in the center of the clearing to glance around at the men, then began shoveling down through what could be a millennium of organic debris, a few feet from the stone pyramid. I was quickly soaked in the hundred-degree heat, yet whenever the men offered to assist I shook my head.

The sound of the camera shutter clicking drove me, the lust for headlines almost as strong as the desire for discovery. On the sites we'd pursued, e-Antiquity had achieved nearly a fifty percent hit rate, unprecedented for treasure hunters. In total our finds had yielded hundreds of millions of dollars—most of which had been claimed by the governments where the antiquities were found. Yet the string of successes had given us notoriety, and when we took our small company public, investors followed with dreams of exponential riches. They weren't unhappy, but we'd yet to find "the big one."

As I dug, Jack's words haunted me. We'd bet the farm on El Mirador, and now my Chaos theory had diverted our team into virgin territory.

"You're four feet deep, Buck," Cody said.

"That should equate to approximately a thousand years of organic sediment," Scarlet said.

More camera clicks followed, and all I could see at my eye level were people's feet. When I stopped for a breather Cody handed me a bottle of water.

"Anything?" he said in a low voice.

I shook my head.

"Want me to dig for awhile?" Cody said.

I shook my head again, unable to speak.

After twenty more minutes of digging, a quiet chant sounded in the air around the hole. It took me a moment to understand what the group was yelling. When I did, though, the chill that ran down my spine and arms made me fumble the shovel.

"Buck! Buck! Buck! Buck!"

The encouragement revived my numb limbs, and before long I was up to my neck in black dirt. My hole had narrowed, and root matter, leaves, worms, and dirt had been the sole product. As if through a tunnel, I heard Scarlet's voice.

"No rocks or other antiquities in the hole proves that all the fill's organic, and the deeper Buck goes without hitting rock, then the older the—"

CLUNK.

My shovel hit something hard, sending a shock wave through my tired body. I'd been so committed to my Alnilam theory that I was willing to dig to China to prove it right.

God, please, let this be something important.

I thrust my shovel forward—

CLUNK!

Again—

CLUNK, CLUNK, CLUNK.

Every attempt in a three-foot radius met with solid rock.

"You want help, Buck?" Cody said.

"Throw me a broom."

Using the broom, then my hands, I exposed gray rock. It was the color of the limestone Mayan structures. By itself, it meant nothing.

Exhaustion and self-doubt threatened. Voices called out from the rim of the hole, asking what I saw. I continued digging, scraping, and brushing away dirt, hoping for something to report—

A circular mark appeared on the stone below me. I brushed a wider circle around it and found more carved lines—I swallowed—more lines appeared. Then the lines came together into a tight angle, with other subtler lines. Teeth.

The rock I'd begun to uncover had a squinted eye and a mouth baring teeth!

"Something's here!"

There was a scramble above me.

I climbed out of the hole, now more than seven feet deep, and without a word our excavation team jumped right in. They barraged me with questions and the photographer clicked away, but I couldn't yet speak coherently, both exhausted and desperate with thirst. Scarlet handed me water, and everyone waited until I looked up.

My face had to be covered in dirt, but my smile created a domino effect of smiles.

"I'm very confident…that I've just made…a major…discovery."

The journalist from *National Geographic* shouted, "Why so confident?"

I dropped to one knee and used a stick in the dirt to sketch out the carving I'd found—a serpent's head with exposed fangs.

"You recognize that?"

"The symbol of Reino Kan?" the journalist from the *National Geographic* said.

"Very good. The Serpent King was the supreme leader of El Mirador at the height of the city's strength. We know no details about his death or his heirs' deaths, but we know their dynasty flourished between 600 BC and 100 AD."

When I stood up, I was looking down at the chunky journalist, shifting his weight from foot to foot.

"Wasn't long after that," he said, "the Mayan people lost faith in the leaders here at El Mirador and abandoned the city."

I nodded, appreciative that he'd done his homework. That meant he'd write a meaningful article on whatever we were about to find. The sound of multiple shovels scraping against rock rose from the hole like smoke from a chimney.

I went on to elaborate. "My hypothesis is that the people lost faith and left because the king, or his heirs, took the wealth with them when they died. I'm banking on the treasury, as I've referred to it, being buried with the Serpent King—"

"Buck!" It was Cody. "We found an edge to the stone!"

Back down in the now six-foot-wide hole, I knelt to examine the gap Cody had discovered a foot from the edge of the dirt wall.

"Use that pry bar," I said, "and give it all you've got."

Two of our Guatemalan crew got in position as Cody and I crawled up out of the way. I gave them the signal and they leaned into the pry bar—the stone moved! They tried again, it lifted a few inches—BOOM! It crashed back down.

I jumped back into the hole and added my weight to the lever—my guts feeling as if they'd split wide open—the stone lifted—dust shot out from inside as if the space below had been filled with compressed air. We shifted our weight to the right and the stone walked with us—

Cody yelled, "Another foot over!"

"BUCK! BUCK! BUCK! BUCK!"

Louder now, the chant made me clench my teeth and press harder.

"That's good!" Cody said.

We slowly lowered the seal stone, and I could feel my heart pounding in my jugular vein. The chasm below was a dark void.

"Throw me a light!"

Scarlet slid down the side of the hole holding a light in each hand. She was breathing heavily.

"What do you think?" she said.

"Smell that?" I said.

Her nose quivered like a mouse catching wind of cheese.

"Putrefaction. This tomb's been closed tight."

Scarlet broke into the biggest smile I'd ever seen on her face.

"Let's kick some serpent ass," I said.

Lying on my stomach, I pointed the light into the depths of the hole—bright colors adorned the walls of the expansive chamber. Reds, yellows, greens, blues, painted images that seemed as fresh as the day the crypt was sealed. The bottom of the chamber was only about eight feet down. I hung onto the edge, silently counted to three, and dropped in—THUMP! I hit and rolled to my right, thudding into something solid.

I shined the light forward—it *was* a cavern.

And it wasn't empty.

Scarlet called down. "What d'you see?"

It took me a minute before I could say anything.

"Come on, I'll catch you!"

She lowered her feet, and I was able to grab her ankles and guide her onto my shoulders. Her light beam slashed through the darkness—

"My God, Buck!"

Dirt rained down from above as Cody and the journalists dropped into the hole, then lowered themselves into the chamber. Each one had the same reaction, if not expressed in the same words.

"Holy crap!" said the photographer from *National Geographic*.

"What the hell?" said the journalist from the *Times*.

"¡*Querido Dios*!" the local reporter said.

The observer from the University of Central America just stared, open-mouthed.

"Son of a bitch!" Cody said.

All our light beams caught on the mummified remains of what I fully expected to be Reino Kan and three other men, all ornamented in brightly covered shrouds, no doubt buried at different times in the family tomb. After a moment I aimed my light past the dead kings into what was a shockingly deep chamber, all of it with the same brightly painted red walls, ornately decorated with images of El Mirador in its heyday. La Danta appeared central and regal. But there were also illustrations of men fighting—many men—an historic detail of war.

"The walls are so brilliant," the journalist from *National Geographic* said.

"Painted with the blood of virgins," I said.

The sound of his mouth sucking air made me smile.

Everyone fell silent.

When we aimed our lights deeper into the cavern a collective gasp broke the silence. Piles and piles of antiquities and riches—gold, obsidian, fabrics, pottery, weapons, more gold, silver, jewels—were piled several feet deep to the end, some fifty feet away. It was a blur of valuables that the king, or kings, had sought to take with them into their afterlife.

"The treasury." Scarlet's voice was a whisper.

"Yeah!" I pumped my fist. "Yeah, yeah, yeah!"

Scarlet and I laughed—embraced—and danced a jig while the photographer's flash strobed staccato shadows onto the bloody walls. Cody jumped between us and the three of us spun around shrieking and laughing until tears filled my eyes.

"You did it, Buck!" Cody said.

6

THE FAST-TRACK DOCUMENTATION PROCESS TOOK THE balance of the day. A complete photographic summary was made of each inch of the chamber, the position of the mummies, the endless pile of antiquities, the juxtaposition of each item to the next closest one, all of which was measured, recorded, and codified in triplicate. Scholars from the University of Central America hemmed and hawed like teenagers at an orgy, all of it lost on me since I spoke no Spanish.

Nobody, including me, expected the cache to be this vast. Fortunately, we'd negotiated an expedited extraction plan with the government for whatever we found.

The academicians, scholars, and the journalist from *National Geographic* argued against the removal of any item from the chamber, but my agreement was ironclad, negotiated by New York attorneys, translated into Spanish, and signed by the president of Guatemala himself, Ramón Garcia. Nobody liked it, but while we'd been painstakingly documenting the chamber, Cody and the rest of my team had been setting up the winch-and-pulley system, preparing airtight storage cases, clearing jungle, and erecting a small village of processing tents where we could quickly yet thoroughly process each item from the underground treasure trove.

The ratio of pottery, tools, and mementoes versus gold objects, gods, amulets, jewelry, and crudely fashioned silver bars was skewed toward the latter, which none of us had ever imagined—nobody had. Even better, two detailed, immaculate codices were found under the largest mummy. We assumed the Serpent King himself had chosen these documents from all the treasure and royal possessions of the pre-classical Mayan dynasty to be buried directly under his remains.

That discovery had everyone salivating, and even though it was a thousand years older than the Dresden Codex, which was believed to have been discovered by Hernán Cortés in 1519 and translated by Dresden librarian Ernst Förstemann 350 years later, we hoped that his key would be applicable here. The information had the potential to explain many missing details of Mayan history, which could make the codices more valuable than all the other treasures we'd packed and delivered through the hole in the roof.

Once the extraction was complete, everyone who'd been below ground climbed up the ladder and into the twilight. I stayed behind and slowly wandered around the now vacant chamber. The wall paintings told stories that were both fascinating and well preserved.

The ladder creaked, and over my shoulder I saw Scarlet step off the last rung. We'd been on enough successful excavations that she didn't ask what I was doing. Instead, she stood next to me and we both stared at the walls, observing the details, soaking it up for one last moment.

"You did it, Buck. Against all odds, and with no basis in known history, you not only found the Serpent King and his heirs but illuminated an entirely different reality about Mayan history." Her eyes glistened in the dim, dry grotto.

"You know e-Antiquity's stock will go crazy," I said.

She took a small step back. "That's it?" An edge lifted her voice.

"Everything you said is true, but it'll also catapult e-Antiquity to rock-stardom both on Wall Street and with every archeological society on the planet."

A chill passed over me, and I suddenly couldn't wait to speak with my father—both my parents, but especially my dad.

"So this is just about money for you?" she said.

"Not at all, Red. Think of the other discoveries this'll lead to. I'm not sated, baby, I'm just getting started."

She came close and hugged me, while I wanted to get up the ladder and inspect the antiquities in the daylight. When she turned her face up to kiss me, my lips brushed hers, then I stepped aside.

"Let's go see the fruits of our labor."

I climbed the ladder without looking back.

7

"WE DID IT, DAD! WE FOUND THE SERPENT KING!"

"Congratulations, son! We had every… confidence in you." His voice breaking meant he was tearing up with excitement. He put the phone on speaker, and my mother and brother Ben were all on the line.

"Wait until you see the cache that was buried with the king."

Dad said, "Did you find it under one of the pyramids?"

"No, I had an epiphany about the main boundaries of the former city and extrapolated the location of the structures as they related to the same configuration in the constellation Orion."

"Your theory proved true." My mother's voice was a whisper.

"And?" Ben said.

"We found—" my voice cracked "—the treasury."

They cheered so loud I had to hold the phone away for a minute.

"There's something even better," I said.

Once I described codices that might contain clues to unknown aspects of the pre-classical Mayan period, they were even more interested than they'd been in the treasure. I promised to call when we arrived back in the States, then I dialed the next number—Jack Dodson's direct line.

Katie, his assistant, answered. "There was just a news story on you!"

Crap. Jack'll be pissed. Jack Dodson didn't like to be anything other than first to know things.

She transferred me.

"Buck! What the hell's going on down there?"

"Sorry, buddy, just got out of the hole a little while ago—"

"It's sensational! The stock jumped thirty percent this afternoon. The photos they're running on TV show a ton of booty, man. Well done! Any guess of the value?"

"The professor from the University of Central America said he thought it would be worth at least a hundred million, but I'd guess closer to a hundred and fifty, easy. But with the historic information and the pair of codices we found, it's impossible to quantify the esoteric value of what'll be learned."

"Damn straight, brother." He paused for a breath. "In our wildest dreams watching Indiana Jones movies, we never dreamed of this, did we?"

"Hell, I sure did."

He laughed. "Give Scarlet a hug for me, then get your ass home with our cut. We'll be planning a hero's welcome and PR campaign that'll have every school kid checking the Internet to learn about Buck Reilly. Indiana *who*? Ha!"

Scarlet walked into the tent as I hung up.

"Enjoy this moment, Buck. You'll be a legend, and richer than you already are." Her eyes turned away from mine, and I thought I saw her wince.

"But?"

Her chest rose as she inhaled. "But… when someone's on top of the heap, a lot of people hope to see them fall. Human nature, jealousy, envy, call it whatever you want, but people like to see champions fail."

"Or repeat their success. Fans love dynasties." I winked at her. "Don't worry, Red, I can handle it. Plus, nothing can end this run. Man, e-Antiquity will be too big to fail."

"If you say so." She grabbed my arm. "Come outside, I have an idea."

Directly overhead, the afternoon sun lit the brilliant mountain of Mayan treasures like a bonfire against the brown-and-green jungle. The clearing was packed with tables where each piece was being minutely described, photographed, and tagged. I walked around the site, absorbing it all, speechless.

And proud.

The *Times* photographer took endless pictures, and as I approached the pile he turned his camera on me. Scarlet was providing the journalists with public-relations quips about e-Antiquity, and when she saw me coming she waved me closer to lead me to the pile.

"Climb into the middle of that mound of history for a picture."

Everyone stopped what they were doing to watch as I stood there, studying the pile, searching for a place to step up. Someone must have thought I was being hesitant.

One voice started: "Buck! Buck! Buck!…"

In a moment, every person there, English speaking or not, joined in the chant.

"BUCK! BUCK! BUCK!…"

I picked my way into the pile, careful not to disturb anything, until I was surrounded by the most valuable ancient treasure trove discovered in modern history. *Ever* discovered, so far as I knew. I found a small table in the center and cleared it off to kneel on, making it look to the photographer as if I sat atop the pile.

The photographer moved in—

"Wait!" Scarlet said.

She rushed over to one of the aluminum cases in the shade of the tent that held the fiberglass coffins and came jogging back holding a gold crown.

"Put this on."

It was the crown we'd found next to the Serpent King. I studied it for a moment while the auto-shoot on the camera rattled away—the gold was brilliant, and there were jeweled ornamental snakes and serpents around the headband, with four loops that connected in the center above it.

"Go ahead," she said, "put it on."

The crown was too small for my head, so I balanced it on my scalp. Of course the professional photographer captured the moment, while many of our team snapped shots on their cell phones. Joy poured over me like warm honey.

"King Buck!"

Scarlet's voice carried from behind the journalists, and I saw them scribbling notes. The sound of the camera shutter was like a machine gun pointed directly at me.

"KING BUCK, KING BUCK, KING BUCK…"

From my seat amid the pile my skin tingled with the very sensation of power fueled by adrenalin that Reino Kan must have felt wearing this same crown.

"KING BUCK, KING BUCK, KING BUCK!"

8

30 DAYS LATER, NOVEMBER 2006

"IT IS THE DISTINGUISHED HONOR OF THE EXPLORERS' CLUB Board of Directors to bestow our highest award, the Explorers' Club Medal—its other recipients having included Admiral Robert Peary, Neil Armstrong, Sir Edmund Hillary, and Jane Goodall, among a select few—to Charles B. Reilly III, or, as he is now known, King Buck."

The president of the Explorers' Club, Sir Andrew Carswell of Edinburgh, Scotland, was known around the world for his studies of ancient habitats of Picts and Gaels in his native land. Of modest height, with close-cropped gray hair and trim beard, along with his buttery Highland brogue he brought Sean Connery to mind.

"History has been rewritten, thanks to you, Buck," he continued once the applause died down. "And once the ancient texts from the forty-one-page Reilly Codex are broken, God only knows what else will be learned." The twinkle in his pale-blue eyes made it clear he was enjoying the moment.

Our hope—Jack's, Scarlet's, and mine—that the same language from the Dresden Codex would work here hadn't panned out. More than a thousand years older, what I'd referred to earlier as the El Mirador Codex—now renamed for me, one of dozens of honors heaped on me since my return from Guatemala—was far more primitive than the Dresden Codex.

"Ladies and gentlemen, I give you Charles B. Reilly III."

When the crowd of approximately a hundred and twenty people jumped to their feet, the volume of applause set me back on my heels. My parents were in the front row (my mother wiped away a tear), Jack Dodson was there (he wolf-whistled), and Scarlet, in a long emerald-green gown with a gauzy shawl around her shoulders, smiled big.

It was nearly Thanksgiving and chilly here in New York City. There were two empty seats in the front row, the only ones in the room—one for me, the other with a name tag I couldn't read.

"Thank you very much," I said. "Do please be seated."

The applause continued for another full minute before everyone sat down.

"It is my honor to accept the Explorers' Club Award on behalf of everyone at e-Antiquity, including my lifelong friend, partner, and co-founder Jack Dodson, our amazing team of world-class researchers and archeologists, and especially Scarlet Roberson and Cody Jacobson, all of whom are present tonight." More applause.

"And let me assure you that none of this would have been possible without our visionary investors, several of whom are here as well, and, in Guatemala, colleagues at the University of Central America, others at the Ministry of Culture, and President Ramón Garcia, who gave our team unprecedented access and rights. The majority of the antiquities discovered at El Mirador, including the Serpent King and his heirs, will be on permanent display at the National Museum of Archeology and Ethnology in Guatemala City. The government expects the volume of tourism—"

At the back of the room, as a door swung open, several people craned their necks to see who had the bad taste to enter so late. A tall blonde woman in a dazzling black low-cut gown strode down the aisle with all the poise and confidence of a runway model.

No wonder, for she *was* a model—in fact, a supermodel.

Heather Drake's eyes locked onto mine as if no other people were in the room. Of course most of those in the room were watching her walk, many of them recognizing her from magazine covers, TV commercials, and advertising campaigns. Her bright-red lips curved upward in a smirk, and she marched to the front row and stopped at the seat next to mine—so that's who it was reserved for. Before sitting down, she gathered the long slit up the side of her tight skirt and lowered herself elegantly onto the chair.

When I saw my father waving his hand in a circle, I realized I hadn't uttered a word since she'd entered the room.

"As I was saying..." I paused to clear my throat. "What exactly *was* I saying?"

Laughter broke out, mostly amongst the men. Scarlet wasn't even smiling.

I pulled the notes from my tuxedo pocket, caught my breath, and spoke for another ten minutes on how e-Antiquity had donated eighty percent of the El Mirador find to the Guatemalan people. I then launched into the canned PR portion of the speech, written by Jack and Scarlet, to thrill and attract investors, provide sound bytes for media, and nauseate me.

Once finished, I replaced the notes in my pocket.

"And now, it's my pleasure to introduce Scarlet Roberson, who will present a slide show including several previously unseen photographs from inside the hidden chamber—"

Applause drowned out my final thank-you, and as I stepped away from the podium and my eyes again locked with Heather Drake's, I collided with Scarlet. She had walked toward the stage when I turned awkwardly in her direction. Her eyes darted from mine to Heather's before she spun on her heel and took command of the lectern.

Whether the applause continued for me or for Scarlet I wasn't sure. In my mind it was only white noise, because my attention was fixed on the brilliant smile and cute, slightly upturned nose of Heather Drake, who leaned against me when I took my seat next to her.

"Congratulations, Buck—may I call you that? Or do you prefer King Buck now?"

Our handshake lingered, and she slowly wrapped her other hand around mine. Her grip was warm and steady.

"Funny—and I recognize you—Heather."

If possible, her smile grew even wider.

The lights dimmed and I vaguely heard Scarlet's voice as her slides flashed on the screen and the audience oohed and aahed. She led everyone through a comparison of the constellation Orion with a map of El Mirador, then started with what I knew to be twenty slides from the chamber.

"So thrilling." Heather's whisper tickled my ear.

"Did you come just for this?"

"Especially this—I'm a member, you know."

"You're a *member* of the Explorers' Club?"

"Ssshh!" I looked up to see my mother pointing toward Scarlet.

"Honorary member, that is. My great-great-grandfather was Sir Edmund Hillary. But I do love to wander off the beaten track."

"...And when Buck hit the top of the chamber in the bottom of the hole..." Scarlet's voice seemed very distant.

"Very impressive, Buck. To get the Explorers' Club's highest honor—all of the honors that you've received this past month—*truly* amazing."

She was so close to my face when she spoke, her breath was warm on my lips, her scent intoxicating. Heather was tall, I guessed five-eleven, but I had to hunch my six-foot-three frame down to hear her above Scarlet's presentation—shit!

I glanced up to find Scarlet staring at me as she spoke, her voice flat, clicking through the slides quickly. Her eyes held mine in a long glare.

Oh jeez.

"I'm in New York for the next few days," Heather said. "Are you available?"

My attention shifted from Scarlet back to Heather, to see that she'd once again donned the smirk that turned her lips up at an adorable angle.

"I have some investor meetings and another couple of events like this, but yeah, as a matter of fact—"

Applause commenced, and the lights came up. Scarlet's show was over. She paused at the lectern, nodding at the crowd, and I'd known her long enough to recognize the tightly clenched jaw and flaring nostrils. She was angry, or at least upset. She stepped away from the podium, and I watched as she walked past, ignoring me to continue down the aisle and out the door.

Damn.

Everyone stood, and Jack Dodson came over. He gave Heather a hug.

He leaned in close to me. "Thought you two might have some things in common."

I looked him in the eye. "You know each other?"

"I have to live vicariously through you, partner."

"You chose to get married in college."

"Because Laurie wouldn't—"

"I remember, Jack." I didn't want to hear him complain that his then girlfriend, now wife, refused to have an abortion after he got her pregnant. He'd grown increasingly bitter ever since.

Heather gripped my biceps. "Will you escort me to the bar? I'd like a glass of champagne."

With each deep breath I could feel my own smile get broader.

"I'd like that," I said.

Champagne turned into an invitation to take her back to her hotel, the Ritz-Carlton, and her limo driver hadn't driven us a block before she stretched her long legs over mine and pulled me close. We came at each other like pit bulls, clashing teeth as our lips pressed together in a frenzy. I pulled her bare legs closer, my hand slipping up to cup her rear end—she wasn't wearing any underwear.

The screech of the car's brakes barely broke through our fervor. When the hotel doorman opened its back door we nearly tumbled out, now laughing hysterically. Once outside, I straightened my tie. Heather grabbed and yanked my hand as we entered, and with long strides we passed quickly through the lobby. Several people recognized her, one recognized me, and the elevator opened the moment she pressed the illuminated button. I could relate.

The doors hadn't fully closed when she spun into my arms—our lips again pressed tight enough to bruise—and when the elevator opened we were in her penthouse suite. Heather's chest rose and fell with her breathing in quick cadence as our eyes locked together.

"I flew over from Italy this morning," she said, "just to meet you."

I rested my hands on her silk-covered hips. "Was it worth it?"

"Too soon to say."

When I bent down to kiss her, softly this time, she pulled me in tight. Time stood still as the urgency of our embrace built, and she led me deep into the suite, past a fluffy white bed where candles flickered from side tables, then on into the bathroom where another candle sent our long shadows onto the tile walls. She turned on the shower.

"I'm feeling dirty," she said.

The dress fell from her shoulders, and she was completely naked. She stepped backward into the stream of water, sending rivulets flying, their candlelit silhouettes stirring an image in my mind of an exploding volcano. I pulled my clothes off and as I moved into the heat, our lips connected, I then strayed down her neck and torso, her nipples springing to my tongue. She leaned against a handrail with one leg lifted and toes clinging to a shelf. She pulled me forward—and in seconds I could no longer tell where my body stopped and hers began. A wail escaped her parted lips as hot water pounded my chest, but it was nothing compared to the cauldron of our connection. My back arched and I was lost unto her, in oh so many ways.

9

MAY, 2007 SIX MONTHS LATER

Blue water raced beneath us as the Cessna Citation CJ4 jet bounced in mild turbulence above the Sir Francis Drake Channel.

Heather's voice sounded in my headset. "The colors are like a Bonnard painting."

My mind was focused on the landing checklist.

The twin Williams FJ-44-4A turbofan engines that together produced more than 3,600 pounds of thrust made this business jet a dream to fly. As we descended from the 27,000-foot cruising altitude toward the Virgin Islands, Heather called out each island she recognized.

"There's St. Thomas." She pointed. "And St. John." She pointed to the right, then swung her hand over to the left. "And that's Jost Van Dyke over there." Then she turned toward me. "And you're still not telling me where we're going?"

"Citation N1745 requesting permission to land at Terrence B. Lettsome Airport," I said.

Air Traffic Control responded.

"Tortola, huh?" Heather said.

"Not our final destination. But I need to focus on landing."

She slapped my shoulder. "You know I love surprises."

We'd been inseparable since that first steamy night in New York, with her joining me at other awards banquets, me hanging out with her at fashion shoots. I'd been shocked when paparazzi began to follow us and our pictures started appearing in the gossip rags I'd always ignored. Part of me was mortified, another part thrilled. The attention had impelled us to take several trips to avoid the barrage of press, including New Year's weekend in a beachfront bungalow at Pink Sands Hotel on Harbour Island, and a weeklong escape to St. Barth's where visitors and residents alike turned blind eyes to celebrities.

I'd come to know Heather in a way I'd never known any other woman. Aside from her extraordinary beauty and her inexhaustible sex drive, she was impetuous, spontaneous, irrepressible, and smart as a whip, even if she was out for herself. She was a supermodel, after all. But she was also the only person I'd ever met who'd made a perfect score on her first try at the SAT exam, leading to a full scholarship at Harvard, which she abandoned after the first semester when a top New York modeling agency discovered her at winter break. She freely admitted the quick cash of modeling was more appealing than years of college.

We descended below ten thousand feet. I reduced speed to 280 knots and flipped on the landing lights. Virgin Gorda passed off our port wing. ATC vectored us closer, and I reduced our speed to 180 knots. With the runaway lined up ahead, I added more flaps, further reduced speed to 130 knots, and we dropped down toward Runway 25. The moment we touched down—softly—I lowered the nose wheel, deployed the spoilers, used reverse thrust until we slowed to 60 knots, then applied the manual brakes.

"Nice landing, captain," Heather said.

We taxied to the private aviation hangar to deplane, and porters took our bags to Customs where I'd prearranged priority clearance. We were whisked through to a blue Ford Crown Victoria waiting for us outside. A man about sixty-five years old jumped out.

"Welcome to Tortola! I'm Valentine Hodge. Pleasure to meet you, King Buck!"

While Heather wasn't used to playing second fiddle, she never once complained about it. She saw me smirk and blew me a kiss.

"Okay, lovebirds," Valentine said, "your boat's waiting in Road Town."

"Boat?" Heather said.

"No questions."

The drive was smooth and quick. Valentino regaled us with stories of Tortola until we pulled up to a dock at the Road Town harbor with a sign that had Heather squealing in delight.

"Peter Island, huh? Nice." She pinched my ass.

Two uniformed men loaded our bags—two for me, four for Heather, plus her mammoth Prada purse. We boarded the fifty-foot yacht, staffed by a captain and two stewards, and commenced the four-mile ride to Peter Island. The sun was high in the cloudless sky, salt air stuck to my exposed skin, and the water shimmered like glass. Tortola faded to a mass of green hills sandwiched between sky and water, both so clear it gave the sense of a reflection.

We sat in chairs on the rear deck and sipped rum punches. The rush of air from the boat's speed was so loud we had to shout to hear each other. Nothing spoke of freedom more to me than being on the water in the Caribbean. I'd been around the world several times over on archeological trips and before that on my father's State Department business, but the joy I felt in the islands was incomparable.

Which is why I'd brought Heather here.

I caught her staring at me, a Cheshire cat grin pulling at her lips. We held hands, and even though I knew the scenery around us was breathtaking, I couldn't take my eyes off her.

Within an hour we arrived at the marina and were transferred to our beach-front suite. While a uniformed man wrestled with our bags, we went outside to find a private hot tub and two lounge chairs overlooking an amazing white-sand beach.

By the time the porter had carried the last two bags inside, Heather had my shirt off and was working on my shorts, with me fending her hands off. When I heard the door close I released her hand, which went immediately to work as I unzipped her one-piece whatever-it-was to fall to the stone patio simultaneously with my shorts. There were people at the far end of the beach, so I took her hand and led her into the hot tub where nobody could see us. On the seat there, we stared into each other's eyes like a challenge to see who blinked first, while our hands delicately caressed, pulled, and probed. She suddenly curved her back, closed her eyes, dropped her head back—she let out a moan that I was sure had been heard back in Tortola.

So focused on her, I didn't realize how hard I was until she slid on top of me and slowly raised herself then eased down in the hot water, until I too felt the jolt of pleasure—she whimpered again, and I opened my eyes to see her head back so far that the tips of her long blond hair dangled in the water.

We lay next to each other in the shallow tub, naked, the sun beating down on us, drained and relaxed. My heart didn't stay calm for long, however. My plans were already in motion, and Heather's surprises had only just begun.

10

Dinner was served under a palm tree on Little Deadman's Beach. The name of the sandy spit gave me a shiver. Two waiters kept our drinks fresh, mine Cruzan Single Barrel Rum on ice, Heather's a Cosmopolitan. The sunset scorched the horizon over our shoulders into a mix of fruit colors, which reflected and sparkled on the slow waves lapping the shore just a few yards from our feet.

"You're a bad influence on me, Buck Reilly. I'm cancelling way too many modeling assignments. My agent says people will stop requesting me."

"Oh, yeah, that'll happen. Stop booking the most beautiful woman on the planet."

"I haven't worked this little since I started in the business."

"And I haven't neglected e-Antiquity this much since we went public. Jack's freaking out because Scarlet quit, and he wants to know when I'll be back—"

"You're King Buck, you don't need to work."

As if on cue, my cell phone chimed and I saw it was a text from Jack. "How's it going so far?"

I turned the phone off.

Our chatter turned to what we'd do over the next few days, which islands we loved, diving, beach-hopping, maybe shopping in Charlotte Amalie, but all the while my heart had been pounding an extra beat faster, my palms sweating, and my mind off in a distant land I'd never explored but was preparing myself to enter. I nodded to our waiter, who promptly produced an ice bucket of Crystal champagne.

"What have we here?" Heather said. Her smile caught the sunset, and her eyes twinkled. "You know I love champagne—"

POP!

Our glasses were filled, and not a drop was spilled. I raised my glass.

"And you know that I love you, Heather."

"Aww, come here, babe." She leaned forward and kissed me gently. "I love you, Buck, so much that it scares me."

Her eyes became serious for a moment. She glanced away but then turned back, her lips pursed.

"I don't want you to be scared, in fact—" I cleared my throat, lurched forward and off my chair while reaching into my pants pocket—

"Buck? What're you—Buck!"

She saw the black square box in my hand as I lowered myself to one knee.

"I want to keep you safe, happy, and with me for the rest of your life. For *both* our lives." I hesitated, loving the anticipation on her face, the quick rise and fall of her chest—the smile I longed to see.

"Will you marry me, Heather?"

The box opened with a snap, and the torchlight beside the table lit the four-carat diamond ring in an explosion of dazzling brilliance.

I held my breath, my eyes fixed on hers, which rose from the ring to focus on my face. She slid off the chair, knelt next to me, and when she wrapped her arms around me we rolled onto our sides, laughing.

"Yes, Buck Reilly! I *will* marry you!"

We held each other in a tight embrace, sand on our arms, legs and down our clothes, and with tears in our eyes. Neither of us could speak through the rush of emotion. My hands shook, both at the enormity of what was happening but also because I wasn't done with surprises just yet. I stood and pulled her up with me.

"I have another question for you," I said.

She leaned back but hung onto my shoulders, eyes wide.

"Will you marry me here, tomorrow?"

Her jaw fell open.

"Buck? My family—our families, what about—"

I looked past her and waved.

She spun around to see her mother, followed by her father, and my parents and brother emerge from the restaurant, and as they walked toward us on the sandy path, her mother started running. Heather dove into her embrace, followed by her father, who wrapped his arms around them both. My own parents scrambled past and met me halfway, both of them sobbing—as were Heather's parents. We all hugged and couldn't speak.

My brother had a serious look on his face.

"Why all the crying?" Ben asked me. "Did she say no?"

Everyone laughed, and since they'd already met each other on the journey down by private plane the day before, there was enough familiarity for hugs, laughter, and more champagne. Our glasses clinked together, all under the starlit canopy.

"Hold on," I said. Everyone turned to face me. I took Heather's hand, the ring again catching the light. "You never answered me."

"Yes I did, I—oh. You were *serious*?"

I nodded.

She took my hands in hers, inched closer, and stared up into my eyes, four inches above hers.

"Yes, Buck, I'll marry you tomorrow, or whenever you want."

"Woo-hoo!" My mother jumped with a fist in the air.

11

A SUNRISE RUN WITH MY BROTHER AROUND THE FIVE-MILE island started very quietly. I couldn't remember the last time we'd done something together, just the two of us. I glanced over at Ben, no expression on his face as he jogged and stared out toward the water.

"I sure never expected this to happen," I said.

"And I can't believe your butt-buddy Dodson isn't here instead of me."

I huffed as I ran. "You're my brother."

I caught his shrug out of the corner of my eye as we continued down the path.

"You always chose him over me, Buck, for as long as I can remember—"

"You mean ever since that stupid fight you had with him ten years ago?"

"Asshole always picked on me—you just laughed."

"You kicked him in the balls—"

"He never fucked with me again."

I laughed. "Guess that's right."

Ben didn't laugh. "And you've ignored me ever since."

We continued to jog down the path. Sweat streaked down my back and chest. We'd had this conversation before, and Ben had never been willing to let it go. Years had passed, and our five-year age difference and life experience created what I saw as a natural distance, especially with me off at college and then going straight to set up e-Antiquity before he even started college. No, we'd never been close, but he carried this grudge like an Olympic torch. I bit my lip as we slogged up a short hill.

"Can I…ask you…for some advice?" My breathing was now labored.

Ben cut a glance over but didn't respond.

"Do you think I should have…had an attorney…prepare a prenuptial…agreement?"

He laughed out loud. "She has to make a ton herself," he said. "It would have soured everything." We ran on in silence for another twenty yards. "You better be sure about this, considering how fast things have happened."

The conversation I'd had with my father came to mind. "Dad pushed for a year-long engagement, but with her modeling schedule and my backlog of e-Antiquity travel…I feel like a soldier preparing to ship out."

That only produced another shake of his head. "Well, it is Heather Drake, after all. And now that you're King Buck…seems like a celebrity kind of thing to do."

The early morning passed in a flash. My father, brother, and I were dressed in khaki linen slacks, with white linen shirts for them and a light blue one for me. I'd purchased matching infinity rings from Cartier that my father, as my best man, had in his pocket. While a huge buffet was prepared at the Deadman's Beach Bar & Grill—a name that continued to ring ironic—we'd ordered a platter of fresh fruit and juices from room service. I managed a couple of pieces of papaya before declaring I wasn't hungry. My father took my orange juice, walked to the bar, and poured in some of the Cruzan rum.

"Liquid courage, son."

He made drinks for himself and my brother, and we spent a moment sitting outside by the hot tub where a flashback of Heather naked yesterday made me smile into my drink.

"Want another one?" Ben said.

"Are you boys drinking?" Mom had come out to join us. She had a radiant glow, offset by an arched eyebrow. She had on a cerulean blue dress with white piping and looked amazing.

Dad leaned forward. "Just one, honey—"

"Don't just one me, Charles Reilly, Junior." She walked over and took the drink out of his hand, gave us a scowl, and then, just as fast, guzzled it. "You didn't even offer me one."

Our laughter broke the moment. She wrapped her arm around my shoulder, pulled me close, and kissed my cheek. Ben brought a chair over for her and she sat between her boys, as she called us.

"Now, Buck, we've already talked about this once, but—"

"Yes, Mother, I'm sure—"

"She's beautiful smart, successful, and all—"

"I love her, Mom. She's all that, yes, but she's fun, spontaneous, has a good sense of humor—"

"Just like you, dear," Dad said.

Her eyes narrowed again. In a house with three males, she'd always been outnumbered, but she'd never let us walk over her. If anything, it made her more determined to ensure that we used our heads, not just our instincts. I felt my cheeks bend in a smile.

"Love you, Mom." I smiled. "I think you'll love her too."

Another hug was followed by a kiss on my forehead.

After a brief drive, our golf cart delivered us to a beautifully manicured lawn next to a small wooden sign denoting Crow's Nest Villa, which stood on a bluff overlooking the blue water to the north. A large black man in a pastor's robe waited next to a trellised arch draped in white lace that billowed in the light breeze.

"That's a serious-looking fellow, Buck," Mom said. "Good thing we're not late."

I swallowed.

We walked across the lawn to where he stood. Nobody else was there and, given his stern expression, a pang of concern hit me that Heather had changed her mind and fled the island. From this vantage point I could see for long distances—no other golf carts.

The man in the black robe smiled. "I'm Pastor Duncan. It's okay, son, everything'll be fine." He placed both hands on my shoulders, and I realized he was nearly as tall as me. The sun glistened off his buffed bald head. He jostled me gently—I lowered my gaze to his eyes.

"Not going to piss yourself, are you, boy?"

I smiled. "No, sir. Provided the bride doesn't stand me up."

A deep chuckle emanated from his diaphragm. "Don't think that's gonna happen." He explained his plans for the service, the suddenness of it all having left no time for us to write our own vows.

"I just want to get married," I said. "That's what matters, right?"

"What matters is what happens after you're married."

"Here they come!" My mom pointed toward the villa at the far end of the lawn. Mrs. Drake walked ahead, with Heather and her father a few yards behind. My bride wore a classical white wedding gown that left me feeling suddenly underdressed in linen slacks and casual shirt.

Two photographers swarmed her like flies at a picnic, and I shook my head. Somehow, my darling, the supermodel, had found a way to capture the moment, not only for us but no doubt the tabloids as well.

What the heck, why not?

A moment later Heather was next to me, her face shrouded by her veil but clear enough that I could see her soft pink lipstick, adorable upturned nose, and that smile that could light up Yankee Stadium.

Pastor Duncan cleared his throat. "We are here on this solemn occasion to join a man and a woman in the sacred vows of matrimony."

His voice continued but my attention was riveted on Heather. It was as if I could look into her soul, and what I saw were bright colors, fields of wild flowers, snow-capped mountains, virgin beaches—

I felt a pat on my arm. "Son?" Dad said.

"I do!" My voice was loud, even to me—everyone burst out laughing.

"I said, repeat after me." Pastor Duncan smiled. "I, Charles Reilly the Third, take you, Heather Drake, as my lawful wedded wife."

I got the words right, albeit my voice was noticeably less steady. He repeated the statement to Heather, whose voice sounded like an angel's in reply. He asked for rings, and my father handed each of us one that we placed on the other's hand when prompted. Momentary silence fell over us all, punctuated only by the sounds of seagulls, a boat in the distance, a clink of cutlery from the Tradewinds restaurant, my own heartbeat—

"By the power granted to me by the government of the British Virgin Islands, and more importantly, as an agent of our Lord and Savior, I now pronounce you husband and wife."

Although not prompted, I lifted her veil, took her in my arms, bent her back just a bit, and delicately kissed her...and kissed her...and kissed her.

"Ahem." Pastor Duncan cleared his throat. "Congratulations to the Drake and Reilly families. It's been my honor to preside here today." He bowed.

"Please, Pastor Duncan," I said, "join us at our wedding feast down at Deadm— er, at the Beach Bar."

Heather and I posed for pictures, and additional golf carts materialized. We took the last cart and followed our families along the bumpy trail, going up and down hills, in some places pointing out amazing views, in others passing through narrow scrub-wood paths. We emerged at the Beach Bar where the staff was lined up waiting for us, and a reggae version of "Here Comes the Bride" played inside the bar. Too bad Jack and his family, Cody and the team, Scarlet—my stomach dropped, she'd quit e-Antiquity a few months ago. Well, I wished our friends could be here to celebrate, but our lives were in the fast lane now, and this is how it would be.

The pastor was waiting outside before we entered the bar.

"May I offer a word of advice?" he said. "Rich people worry so much about making and preserving their wealth that they neglect the word of God. Remember, children, there is no Heaven on earth, and storing up warehouses of wheat and gold may provide comfort in this life yet prevent you from getting to Heaven. God bless you both."

I grinned at him, then dug into my pocket for my money clip and peeled off five hundred-dollar bills.

"Thank you so much, Pastor." I shook his hand and slipped him the bills.

We entered the Beach Bar to the shouts of our family and the management and staff. I glanced back to see that Pastor Duncan hadn't followed us in.

SECTION 2

LEARN FROM THE WRONG THINGS YOU'VE DONE

12

DAYS PASSED, THEY DIDN'T HAVE NAMES. OUR FAMILIES departed after we'd gone island hopping, scuba diving, hiking, and on a helicopter tour around the BVI. Heather and I were finally alone, and we celebrated by making love and lounging on the beach to deepen the mahogany shades of our skin. After a couple more days Heather announced that she had a modeling gig in Puerto Rico and would have to leave for two nights, which worked fine, because the guilt of resting on my Guatemalan laurels had me increasingly on the phone with Jack and Cody, who'd stepped up since Scarlet left.

A local man from Tortola, Stanley Ober, had been calling our offices incessantly. He'd seen the news, knew I was in the BVI, and claimed to have a map of great value that he wanted to sell us. The vast majority of leads of this nature proved to be bogus, but my agreeing to meet with him got Jack off my back, as he could tell investors that I was investigating new opportunities.

Heather and I took the ferry to Tortola, where Valentine Hodge again retrieved us. After we dropped Heather at the airport he drove me to Road Town, where I stopped at

Barclays Bank. Jack had transferred funds so I could have a blank cashier's check with me for the meeting with Stanley Ober. I'd learned long ago that money talks, and bullshit walks.

I'd arranged to meet Ober at Pusser's Outpost, right by the ferry terminal, and as I entered the covered patio, a man waved to me.

"Buck Reilly! Over here." He was a fifty-something local in dark slacks, white shoes, and a green sport shirt. He'd been enjoying a beer and laughing with people at other tables who also appeared to be local.

"Mr. Ober, I presume?"

"Call me Stanley, Buck. I expect we'll be friends by the time we're done here."

He patted me on the back, guiding me toward the chair next to him. I noticed that leaning against his chair was a white tube, the kind posters came in when bought at shopping malls. Most people in possession of rare artifacts of purported high value are concerned with security and often demand to be met in controlled environments. Mr. Ober's drinking buddies watched us closely, clearly aware of the purpose for our meeting. Perhaps this was his idea of Tortola security.

"Before I show you the map, let me explain how I came to have it."

"Provenance," I said.

Ober stared at me, then half-stood and waved to the waitress.

"Bring Buck Reilly some—what'd you call it?"

"A Heineken is fine, thank you."

"Sometime in the fifteen hundreds," Ober began, "when the Spanish was robbing everyone blind in South America and here in the Caribbean, they didn't always have such an easy time of it."

"The British, French, and Dutch took their toll," I said.

"Very true, but so did the Indians. The Spanish flat-out killed 'em on sight, so the Indians—the Caribs, at least, the Arawaks had already got their asses kicked—didn't much like the Spanish. And they knew the Spanish was stealing gold, silver, jewels, women, you name it. Anything that sparkled, whined, or was mined was put on ships and carried back to Spain."

The Heineken was ice-cold and tasted fantastic. Ober was building his story, while I tapped my fingers on the wooden tabletop.

"One of the Spanish galleons had limped into port here after a storm, and according to legend, the crew was sick and weak after getting pummeled all through the islands. Well, they thought they was safe here in what later became Road Town, but what they didn't know was that the last batch of Spanish had slaughtered a bunch of Caribs and taken some of their women when they moved on.

"So, the story goes that when night fell, a group of maybe twenty Caribs paddled out on canoes, boarded the ship, killed every damn person on board, feasted on 'em—they was cannibals, y'know—then loaded their canoes with as much booty as they could carry."

As I sipped my beer I noticed several men at neighboring tables watching in rapture as Ober spoke. I'd heard vague reports in the past of Indians attacking ships, killing crews, taking goods, even cannibalism, so Ober's story had tickled my curiosity. I felt a mild pang gurgle in my gut.

"So the Caribs got away with some treasure?"

Ober flashed a smiled, then shook his head.

"Oh, they didn't get far. A sister Spanish ship arrived in the middle of the night to find their friends slaughtered and half-ate, and they went out hunting with a vengeance. See, they knew it was Indians because of some arrows left in bodies, and hacking wounds from hatchets.

"So while this new bunch of Spaniards was killing any men, women, and children they could find up in the hills here, a few of the Carib men took off in canoes through the Camanoes toward what we now call Virgin Gorda. But their canoes was loaded heavy with treasure, and they didn't get far before they was chased down and shot with long rifles out in the Sir Francis Drake Channel—"

"And the Spanish didn't recover the treasure?"

"Didn't know about it. They was just looking for revenge."

I killed the beer. Ober sat back and drank from his own—ironically enough, his brand was Carib.

He went on to explain that he was a descendent of the earliest slaves brought to Tortola by Sir John Hawkins in the 1650s, before there were any meaningful European settlements here. His ancestors had been destined for Hispaniola, but Hawkins was made an offer by some English farmers on Tortola and sold the slaves on the spot. Ober claimed that his distant relative had befriended some of the local Indians they traded with, and that one had told him of the incident with the Spanish and even the approximate location where it happened. If the valuables were found, they could be used to buy freedom.

"He showed my relative a crude old map from his descendants who'd seen their men killed while fleeing the Spanish, which is how this map was created." He laid his hand on the cardboard tube.

"And why haven't you gone out and found it?"

"I'd like to, believe me, but it's a pretty wide area shown, and I only got this from my grandmother when she died a few months ago."

"God rest her soul," said an older man from an adjacent table.

Ober finally opened the tube and carefully spread the map on the table. It did look old. I could tell by the type of paper that it might have come from the 1600s—Ober had said it was drawn later. It had a series of three marks out beyond what indeed were the Camanoes, which Ober said he assumed identified individual canoes.

"Look, Buck, I can't guarantee anything," he said, "but they's been talk of this incident in these islands for generations. This is the only map and complete story anyone's ever heard of or seen."

"And you're an expert?"

"I never said that, but I've lived here all my fifty-seven years, and my family's been here hundreds more. My grandmother was a hundred and two when she died, and she told the story like it happened last week." He gave me a questioning look. "Since you was on-island, I thought you'd be interested, but if not, others will be."

We then got down to brass tacks.

"This is pretty much my entire inheritance, and sadly, my grandmother left debts to be paid. I need fifty thousand dollars for the map."

"Fifty thousand? Seriously?" While negotiation always started with incredulity, in reality, $50,000 was nothing if what he said was true.

We bickered a little, but he wasn't budging. I recalled Jack's demand that we needed progress to appease investors. Guatemala was old news, Cody and the team were anxious to move on to the next project, and then there was the loss of Scarlet. She was normally the one to oversee the authentication process, but we no longer had that luxury. Ober wouldn't agree to any escrow or deposit, so I thought what the hell and stuck out my hand.

"Cashier's check is fine, Buck. I drew up this bill of sale, too."

"Pretty confident, weren't you, Ober?"

The bill of sale was simple and said it was final, as-is, and non-negotiable. We both signed it, his group of friends looking on with excitement.

"Drinks on Stanley," one said. Everyone laughed.

I rolled up the map, slid it into the tube, and walked with it out to the lot where Valentine waited. I checked my watch and saw that we still had time to get to the FedEx office, where I'd ship the map and agreement back to headquarters for Cody to inspect, preserve, and copy for our third-party authentication team to review.

Valentine was curious. "Whatcha got there in that tube? A Pusser's Rum poster?"

"Something like that."

13

Heather returned to Tortola two days later, just in time for me to get the angry call from Jack stating that the map from Stanley Ober was a fake.

"You were flim-flammed, Buck," he said. "The water in that area's very shallow, and tourist operators dive there a couple of times a day. If there was ever anything there, it's long gone now."

"Crap."

"What the hell happened?"

"Relax, Jack, it was only fifty thousand dollars—"

"No, Buck, I stuck my neck out to analysts and our investors about this. I trusted you, and now I look like a fool with my entire network."

"Ober had plenty of well-crafted details about an incident, some of which I'd heard of before."

"You need to find him and get our money back. Either we make an example of him, or he does of you. And I lose face."

With that Jack hung up on me. The days of our being best friends, co-captains of our winning high-school football team, and partners in a world-class business the two of us had enjoyed building from scratch might never have happened. In spite of the fact that our success and the money my discoveries produced brought in more and more success and more and more money, he only seemed to become more embittered. Even his praise for the huge Mayan find sounded hollow.

Furious, I had Valentine stop at Pusser's Outpost again before we retrieved Heather from the airport. There was no sign of Stanley Ober, but I did recognize a pair of men sitting at a table drinking beer, just as they'd been a few days before.

"I ain't seen him," the man in the plaid shirt said.

"Last I heard, he was in San Juan," the one in the black shirt said.

I said, "You tell that piece of shit I'm going to find him, and when I do, I'll get my money back one way or another."

Silence fell over the patio restaurant. Tourists stared wide-eyed, and the locals just glared at me.

I stormed out and punched my fist into my palm. People on the patio had turned to watch me stomp to Valentine's Crown Victoria.

"Damn, son, somebody piss in your beer?" he said when I got in.

"I'm an idiot! I knew that guy was full of shit!"

Valentine drove on cautiously toward Terrence B. Lettsome Airport, where Heather had likely been waiting for an hour. He was studying me in the rear-view mirror as he drove.

"Local fellow?"

"Local con artist, more like it." I sat up straight. "Name's Stanley Ober, know him?"

A long whistle sounded from the front seat. "Oh yeah, I know Stanley Ober. You're right, too. He's a con artist, petty thief. Conniver. Wish you'd told me who you were meeting—"

"Dammit!"

Local intel. That had always been Rule #1. The rust caused from hanging out with Heather, screwing off—getting married—I'd forgotten that cardinal rule of negotiating. If I'd I just asked my driver—

"Shit!"

Valentine scrunched down in the driver's seat to accelerate toward the airport. Ten minutes later we found Heather sitting on three bags of luggage—hadn't she left with two? Valentine jumped out to grab her bags.

"It's about time—"

With my window open, I heard Valentine's whisper. "Might cut him some slack, Miz Reilly. He's had a rough day."

She climbed inside, her eyes studying me as if she were assessing an alien. Come to think of it, she'd never seen me angry, much less nail-spitting furious. I never spoke a word until we boarded the yacht back to Peter Island except to thank Valentine. Once the boat left the dock, and Heather and I had the ceremonial rum punches in hand, I explained what had happened. I told her Jack was furious, and that somehow I needed to get a line on the shyster to save some face. I felt bad not asking about her gig in Puerto Rico—one of the men had said Ober might be in San Juan—but she didn't pout or whine, and for that I was grateful.

Once back to our beachfront villa, Heather disappeared into the bathroom while I started making phone calls around the Virgin Islands and Puerto Rico, asking anyone I knew about Stanley Ober. I was dialing up a San Juan hotel and felt her arms wrap around my shoulders from behind just as a voice answered, "Casino del Mar."

I held the phone away long enough to ask, "What are you doing?" When I dropped my shoulder, she lost her grip. I turned to see her standing naked behind me, and in the bathroom I could hear water running into the tub. I just shook my head at Heather and got back to the phone.

"Hello, can I help you?" the voice on the phone said.

"Can you connect me to Stanley Ober's room?"

Slam!

The crash of the bathroom door made me jump.

"I'm sorry, sir, there's nobody here by that name."

After another dozen calls with the same result, the room-service dinner Heather had ordered for me had long ago gone cold, and the rum had run dry before I slammed the phone down one last time.

"Nobody knows shit."

Heather had gone to bed.

My Rolex said it was 11:25. Tonight was shot, and odds were that Ober had pissed the money away in a San Juan casino by now. Jack would just have to bullshit the investors about the authenticity of the map. The money didn't matter, and I was madder at myself for being suckered than at Jack's overreaction, or even Ober conning me. Screw it.

Once in bed, when I tried to spoon Heather, she pushed backward with her ass, and not in a welcoming way.

Way to ruin the honeymoon, Buck.

14

I'D DODGED JACK'S CALLS FOR TWO MORE DAYS, AND ON THE morning of our planned return to Tortola where our rent-a-jet waited to take us to Dulles, a loud knock on the door of our villa woke us at dawn.

When I opened the door, scratching my ass through my boxer shorts, I found two men, one in the uniform of the Royal Virgin Islands Police Force, the other in plain clothes but holding a badge in my face.

"Charles Reilly the Third?" the badge holder said.

"Yeah?"

"I'm Detective Bramble." He smiled. "You're under arrest—"

"What the hell?"

"Buck?" Heather came running from the bedroom, pulling a robe on as she ran. "What did—did he say you were under arrest?"

"What for?"

"The murder of Stanley Ober."

Time blurred after Detective Bramble handcuffed me and led me to a police boat. Heather followed along, repeatedly asking what she should do.

"Call Jack—no—call my father at the State Department! Get me a lawyer!"

After that, everything moved at light speed. We crossed back over to Tortola, then to a police station where I was booked, stripped, cavity checked, sprayed off like a dog, then given an orange jumpsuit and shoved into an 8'x10' stone cell to await arraignment.

The stench of urine, puke, and sweat lined the floor and walls, and initials, obscenities, and crude cartoon images were scraped into the grout. The cell was sweltering, and my jumpsuit was soaked in no time. A single narrow window was at an angle that prevented me from seeing out. It provided minimal air circulation but was an effective portal for mosquitoes and spiders. The stone was filthy but cool, so I sat on the floor and leaned against it.

Day turned to night. I'd had no word from Heather, my father, Jack, an attorney—nothing. Sleep came in brief fits, until a bat flew inside the narrow window and circled around as it engulfed mosquitoes. I pulled the thin sheet over my head and prayed for the hundredth time that this was all a terrible nightmare. Morning came and the cell door opened. I jumped up expecting to see an attorney—Detective Bramble was there instead.

"How's the new palace, *King* Buck?"

"Where's my attorney? I want due process—"

"Ha! Due process, that's funny." His eyes flickered with a greater intensity than you'd expect from a police officer's civil righteousness. I found his stance and demeanor challenging, as if he dared me to try something.

"Why're you so angry, Detective?"

He stared at me for a long moment. "Stanley Ober was a friend of mine, Reilly."

Oh, great.

"I'm telling you, I had nothing—"

"Save it for the magistrate, or better yet, the jury. We have plenty of witnesses to prove our case, no matter how many solicitors your wife produces—"

"Is she here? I have a right to see her!"

"You got no rights, big shot, remember that. But yeah, she's here."

There was an armed guard standing behind Bramble in the hall. They led me down to a holding room where we waited until the door we'd entered was bolted shut. Then, a door on the front of the room opened—Heather walked in—I tried to get up—the armed guard pushed me back in my seat.

Heather was pale, her hair windblown, her clothes rumpled. She sat down next to me and tentatively held out her hand.

"Keep your hand back," Bramble said.

When she swallowed, her Adam's apple moved slowly up and down her neck like a mouse through a snake.

I said, "Can we have some privacy, please?"

"This ain't no conjugal visit."

Heather inhaled deeply. "We have three attorneys on board. Jack, your father, everyone—"

I held my hand up. "Okay, good, but not in front of these men, honey."

Bramble laughed. "We're all ears."

"They're waiting on a consultant to be established who's licensed in the BVI."

I slumped back in the seat. Heather bit her lip.

"That should be final tomorrow, and then they can get you in front of the magistrate for a bail hearing—"

"Don't count on it, Reilly." Bramble glowered. "Man with your resources is a flight risk. Hell, we impounded that private jet—"

"It's a rental, dammit!"

Bramble's smug smile caused me to clench my fist.

"Buck, no—" Heather said.

"Come on, Reilly, you want to add assaulting a police officer to your charges? Go ahead, try me."

I closed my eyes and let out a long breath. I'd be here at least another night.

That one more night turned into ten. Charges were pressed, and the magistrate wasn't negotiating. The prosecutor claimed to have multiple witnesses stating that I'd threatened Ober who, as it turned out, had been found floating in the harbor near San Juan with his throat slit. Motions to overturn were denied, and another ten days passed. I'd reviewed every bit of discovery that the prosecution team had shared with my collective counsel, all of which was circumstantial. Either they had something they weren't sharing with us, or their case was pure hearsay. But in the British Virgin Islands, did it matter?

Heather shuttled information in and out to me and, based on her haggard appearance, the strain on her had been enormous. She'd had to cancel multiple contractual modeling obligations in Europe and New York, and she said one client was threatening to sue. Beyond that, she said that the news media, entertainment shows, and gossip rags were having a field day at our expense. It was hell inside the stone cell, and thanks to the miserable conditions and awful food, I'd lost nearly twenty pounds.

Jack Dodson didn't visit, but he'd sent me letters via FedEx, the latest of which said e-Antiquity's stock had dropped forty percent as a result of the charges against me, and the legal bills had already escalated to six figures. I didn't sense malice in this report, just an update of the situation, which I was fighting for my life to remedy. If it continued much longer, there wouldn't be much to return home to—*if* I was successful in beating the charges.

Out of desperation, I wrote a pleading letter to the one person I believed could make a difference but had no idea whether the letter was ever mailed, or how long it would take to arrive. Accustomed to aggressively pursuing anything I set my sights on, the paralysis caused by incarceration, along with my certainty that I was being railroaded regardless of proof or facts, left me curled up on my cot for days.

For the first time in my life, a sense of hopelessness had felled me.

15

Another ten days passed, and my cliché scratches on the wall had added up to twenty-five. Hope and arrogance had dwindled to self-doubt and fits of anxiety-driven shaking. The private detectives I'd instructed my local attorney to hire hadn't produced anything of value, and I concluded they didn't really care—bonus for news or not.

The trial date was set for a month away. I had witnesses to corroborate my alibi of being on Tortola the day of Ober's death. The fact that I'd stayed in my hotel room at Long Bay Beach Club the night he was killed left a fifteen-hour gap, which the police were exploiting. Given the time that had passed, and the time until the trial, my mind had lapsed into something like hibernation.

A clank at the cell door roused me. It was the big guard I called Bubba, the friendliest of the four who rotated throughout the week.

"Got a visitor, Reilly."

I sat up slowly and rubbed my head. Heather had gone back to the States for work, I had no meetings with my attorneys until Thursday, and I was pretty sure this was Tuesday. Bubba must have recognized my confusion.

"Somebody new." His mocha-brown face cracked into a smile. "Pretty fire-head. Come on."

Fire-head? I'd seen some of the court clerks, and one had orange hair, but she wasn't what I'd call pretty. I hadn't met any of my local attorneys, Rolf Johnson's paralegals. What the heck?

Bubba took me into the same room where I'd met with Heather.

"Bramble's not around, so I'll leave you two alone." He winked and closed and bolted the door. A moment later when the bolt slid open on the other door, my jaw dropped, for Scarlet walked in.

Scarlet Roberson, my former research partner and lover. She stopped in her tracks, and I could tell by *her* mouth falling open that I had to look really bad. When she rushed forward to hug me, I felt my ribs compress in her squeeze. She was tan—freckles dotted her nose—and she looked in better shape than I'd ever seen her.

"Scarlet, I...I...you got my letter?"

She nodded, wiping away tears. She led me to the pair of chairs bolted to the floor and we sat down.

I tried to remember when I'd seen her last—at the Explorers' Club—what was it, a year ago? My mind zigged and zagged.

"I've been following your case. It's not going very well."

"The lawyers say—"

"Why is Moskowitz in charge?" she said. "He's e-Antiquity's corporate attorney. What's he know about criminal defense?"

"Jack trusts him—"

"And the outside counsel—I've seen him on TV, he's a buffoon." She sighed. "I've kept in touch with Cody, and he says most of the effort at the office is about keeping investors happy. Jack has him researching new opportunities in what seems like a back-up plan, if you don't win your case."

"Yeah, well, that's Jack. Covering his bases."

"And Heather's on the cover of the new *Vogue*."

I slapped a palm on the metal table. "Can you help me, Scarlet?"

"I'm not sure. But it doesn't seem like anyone else is trying very hard."

A flurry of shivers curled my limbs.

"We were a good team," I said.

"Yeah, we were."

She stared at me for a long time. "You broke my heart, Buck."

I studied the floor where the table was bolted into the concrete.

"I know. I'm—"

"Don't say it, please, just don't." She took in a deep breath. "I came to help you, one last time."

I reached out to put my hand on hers—she pulled it away.

"But to be totally honest, it's a selfish move, too," she said. "The accusations against you have sullied all the work we've done together, including at El Mirador. I want the record cleared for my own sake as well."

She looked me in the eye. "I never saw you act violently, and I can't believe you'd ever kill anyone, especially over a fifty-thousand-dollar fake map. We lost a lot more than that on some other dead ends. I need your permission, in writing, to speak with and help the local attorney."

I struggled to clear my throat, which had temporarily constricted. I'd assumed we had a good legal team and that everyone was working hard, but I knew Scarlet was brilliant. She could be a game changer.

"Thank you, Scarlet. I can't tell you—"

"Then sign this."

She pulled a letter out of her skirt pocket. It provided my authorization for her to consult with Rolf Johnson and help to research and strategize with him. I took her pen and signed the letter. With that she stood up, and so did I. She took a step back, but I moved faster and took her in my arms for a hug. Hot tears streaked down my cheek. When she saw them she broke free, turned away, and moved quickly toward the door.

"Scarlet—"

But she was knocking for a guard, and in a flash she was gone.

16

The next month passed in a blur, and once the trial began, it only took a week for Adam Swain, the director of public prosecutions in the British territory, to make their case against me. A steady parade of witnesses—friends of Ober's I'd seen at Pusser's, both when I bought the map and when I returned there looking for him after finding out he'd swindled me—all said the same thing: "Mr. Reilly said he'd get his money back, one way or another, and he threatened Mr. Ober."

It was as if they'd rehearsed in a group, and, given the kangaroo nature of the legal-justice system I'd experienced so far, I suspected that Detective Bramble had indeed coached everyone. The detective sat at the prosecution's table and glowered at me nonstop. They had no forensic evidence connecting me to Ober's death, nor any evidence that I'd been to Puerto Rico at the time, which made sense because I hadn't. Regardless, there was a lynch-mob mentality in both that courthouse and the local press. Innocent until proven guilty was not a concept I believed they embraced, and I slept less every night after each of those five days until the prosecution rested.

The magistrate gave us the weekend to prepare for our defense, and Rolf Johnson repeatedly asked me the same questions about the depositions from my Tortola driver Valentine Hodge, Peter Island staff, and the Long Bay Beach Club on Tortola where I'd stayed while I waited for Heather at the same time Ober was getting murdered. There were several eyewitness accounts up to the night of his death, when I was holed up in my room with a Do Not Disturb sign on my door, drinking rum and closing out the world, angry over Jack's criticisms, Ober ripping me off, and Heather off on a modeling shoot in the middle of our honeymoon. It left a big hole in my case that had Rolf Johnson stammering, scratching his head, and poring over testimony.

Come Monday, we assembled in the courtroom, and just before the bailiff called the room to order, a messenger rushed in with a small package for Rolf Johnson. He opened the package to find a note and a compact disk. He read the note quickly, with a sharp intake of breath, glanced at me as he sat up straight, then read it again.

"What is it?" I said.

THWACK! He'd slammed his open palm on the table.

Every face in the room turned our way.

"What's in the package?"

Rolf Johnson had a distant stare and hummed to himself, then held up a hand to stop me asking anything else.

The magistrate entered the courtroom, and once we were called to order, he asked for the defense to commence. Rolf Johnson stood flagpole-straight and cleared his throat.

"Your honor, in light of new evidence, the defense calls for the case to be dismissed."

The room burst into an uproar, led off by the director of public prosecutions, and even Bramble was shouting and wagging a finger toward us. With my heart in my throat, I glanced behind me to see concern and shock on the faces of Heather and my parents at the sudden shift away from the iterative defense we'd carefully planned to rebut the prosecution's circumstantial evidence.

"Order! Order!" the magistrate called. He then beckoned the attorneys to approach his bench. Both men rushed forward, with Rolf Johnson passing around the letter and waving the compact disk around like the Holy Grail.

"The court will take a brief recess to consider new evidence. Counsel, come to my chambers." A large man, the magistrate stood and his black robe whipped around in a flourish as he hastily left the bench to disappear through a door, followed by the two attorneys.

The court erupted with loud discussion as everyone speculated on the purported new evidence.

Dad spoke from behind me. "What the hell's going on?"

"I have no idea—he didn't say."

"Quiet over there!" Bramble stared daggers at us.

Ten minutes passed, with the noise level still high. After another ten minutes it had quieted a few decibels, but when the bailiff appeared, a wave of silence fell over the courtroom. The attorneys marched back to their respective tables, neither giving any hint as to what had happened behind the scenes. Both, in fact, looked agitated.

"What—"

My question was quickly snuffed with an abrupt shake of Rolf Johnson's head—I felt his hand pat my knee—while his eyes remained fixed straight ahead. Whatever had been in the letter and compact disk had so rattled both sides that each attorney appeared tighter than a cork in a wine bottle.

Fifteen minutes later, the magistrate emerged to take the bench and bang his gavel.

"In consequence of new evidence produced by the defense, namely, a video recording that shows beyond the shadow of a doubt another man killing Stanley Ober, the Court of the British Virgin Islands hereby drops the case against Charles B. Reilly the Third—"

"No!" Bramble's voice rang out like a rifle shot, and the crowd of locals shouted insults and epithets in all directions.

I was shaking my head. "What the hell happened?"

My family rushed up and hugged me, but my eyes never left Rolf Johnson's, still waiting for an answer.

"Your friend delivered! If I had someone like her, I'd win every case!"

"Scarlet?" I said.

Still seated, he shimmied his shoulders as if he were dancing, cocked his head sideways, and nodded emphatically.

"Who is he talking about?" Heather said.

"My former research partner at e-Antiquity," I said. "She found something?"

Heather's gaze lingered on my face, perhaps to decide whether Scarlet's involvement should concern her—or maybe that was my guilty conscience, since I was so grateful for help from my former lover.

"She saved our case, Mr. Reilly—"

"What—how?" I said.

"After she saw a newspaper article about an unidentified man getting dragged out of El San Juan Casino the day before Ober's body was found, she persuaded the casino's security manager to show her the surveillance footage of the incident. She identified Ober from the pictures I'd given her. More important, his assailant showed up clearly on the video and is a known criminal who runs illegal gambling rackets."

Johnson smiled. "They're issuing an arrest warrant for him now."

My arms flopped to my sides—I slumped forward.

Scarlet had saved my ass.

"The security video was crystal-clear and showed Ober first arguing and then struggling with this criminal. A second camera outside caught the killer dragging Ober to the curb, opening the boot of his car, and stuffing Ober's lifeless body inside. What you might call unimpeachable evidence." He wagged his fingers in the air. "I'll show it to you back at my office."

I was elated. Also exhausted, malnourished, and had lost so much weight while incarcerated that my father and brother had to assist my victory march, each supporting one of my arms. As I passed Bramble, I blew him a kiss.

From behind me, I heard, "Don't be coming back."

"Don't worry." My voice was a whisper.

17

LATE 2007

It took a lot of work with a personal trainer, nutritionist, and my doctor to regain my physical and mental strength. During that time, Heather alternated between trips abroad on assignment to luxuriating with me in the home we bought in Great Falls, Virginia. When she was home we slept late, made love, and I followed the stock-market news like a junkie—soaring one day, dropping the next—while Heather paged through every fashion magazine on the planet.

One morning she came downstairs carrying two of her Louis Vuitton suitcases.

"You've only been home for five days," I said.

"I don't want to leave, Buck, I really don't, but the contract with Prada is unbreakable. Already a lot of A-list clients are saying they'll never work with me again after so many cancellations."

"You'll be in Rome?"

She tried to pinch off the grin, but the corners of her mouth always turned up to give her away.

"And the Dolomites for the snow shots."

"And if there's no snow?" I said.

"You can always count on St. Moritz."

With that, Heather was gone for another two weeks, at least.

And I became addicted to social media. Against the wishes of Jack and our corporate attorney, but to the delight of news analysts and journalists, I filled the vacuum created by Heather's absence with an aggressive campaign refuting the speculation about whether I might have hired Ober's killer, and the chatter about when e-Antiquity might make a new archeological discovery. Boredom mixed with anger and what I considered well-deserved hubris after finding the tomb of the Serpent King fueled the vitriol I spewed back at the naysayers on Twitter and Facebook, peppered with heretofore unseen pictures from Guatemala or new ones of me to prove that I was both fit, able, and indeed planned to reprise my previous successes. My on-line name was @KingBuck, and my tweets and posts occasionally showed up on CNN, CSNBC, or even *Entertainment Tonight*, which I enjoyed at first but found increasingly irritating.

I rarely answered my cell phone unless I saw that it was Heather or my parents. But today, after checking e-Antiquity's stock and noting it was still down more than forty percent from our high, when the phone rang and I recognized Jack Dodson's personal number I punched the green button.

"Hey, Jack. How's it going?"

"When I saw you a few weeks ago you looked and felt like shit. Any idea when you're coming back to work full time?"

"I'm just about ready to dive back in."

"We need to make another run here. Guatemala was a long time ago, and the troops, investors, and Wall Street analysts are all restless."

His voice didn't sound like his old self. My being gone had widened the gap that had grown between us over the past few years.

"How about I come in tomorrow?" I said.

"Whoa, partner, really? Well, I'd—we'd like to plan something to memorialize, ah, your return. How about next week?"

"It's Tuesday, Jack."

"I'm just thinking about morale. I want everyone to get psyched up, and frankly, they want to surprise you."

I let Jack think I'd wait until the next week, but I was ready to get back in the game. And a surprise visit might help me determine the accuracy of the negativity I'd been reading in the press about e-Antiquity.

Up early the next day, I worked out, showered, and put on one of my Hugo Boss suits, a bright red Hermès tie, and polished my favorite Ferragamo loafers. I'd hardly been in the office over the past six months, except occasionally after hours to meet with Jack, and it was important that I came back looking strong, successful, and focused.

Once rush hour was over, I drove the rolling hills of Rt. 193 through Great Falls in my black Porsche 911 Turbo, doubling and occasionally tripling the speed limit without worrying about radar traps or traffic that I couldn't pass—illegally—on the left side of the road. I pulled into the parking garage on Towers Crescent Boulevard and was pissed off to find my reserved space occupied by a BMW 5-series. I found a visitor's spot and parked at an angle taking two spaces.

Asshole move, but today was my day. King Buck was back and ready to kick some ass.

"Mr. Reilly?" Our receptionist, looking astonished, stood up when the elevator doors on the sixteenth floor opened.

"Nice to see you, Sadie."

Beyond her I saw that the board room was full of men and women in conservative attire, poring over binders stacked in the center of the table.

"Who are those people?"

"Accountants, I think," Sadie said.

Seemed early, given that our fiscal year was the same as the calendar year. Rather than go to my office, I made my way toward Jack's corner suite. Along the corridor surprised faces and shouts of my name greeted me, but my mind was on the people in the board room. Jack's door was closed—Katie, his assistant, shouted my name, too—but I walked straight inside.

Jack was standing at the window, phone cradled in his shoulder .

"Hey, stranger," I said.

He bobbled the phone as he turned to face me.

"Buck?" Then into the phone: "Talk to you later, baby."

A brief hug, and we sat down.

"Who're the stiffs in the board room?" I said.

"Accountants from Ernst and Young. Pre-tax evaluation for our quarterly ten-k."

"I don't recall seeing that before—"

"That's because I'm the one minding the store while you're out chasing glory in some romantic location and hunting treasure—which is what we need you to get back in the field to do ASAP."

Jack had aged, with wrinkles on his forehead I didn't remember, but he was still lean, having been an avid fitness freak ever since his quarterback days on our high-school team. He tapped his fingertips together as we caught up—a few of our people had quit, and a few had been laid off to keep our costs in check.

"Shame that Scarlet's gone." Jack tilted his head. "Did I hear she found the evidence to absolve you in Tortola?"

"Puerto Rico, actually, but yes, and it damn sure sucks that she's gone."

"It does."

"What about Cody?" I said.

Jack reached for his coffee mug and took a sip. "Out in the field—Mexico—researching what we hope will be our next big find."

My stomach twisted. "Is it a dig?"

"No, just research. He's at the Mexican General Archive in Mexico City." He leaned back to stare me straight in the eye. "Cody's really stepped up and should be ready to fill Scarlet's shoes—well, mostly—on your next dig."

I got the message.

Jack stood, walked around his desk and closed his door, then came and perched on the edge of the desk close to me.

"So, Buck, we couldn't really talk before, given the circumstances." He leaned closer. "However much of a nightmare as Tortola was for you, Ober's demise was a good thing."

I sat back. "What's that supposed to mean?"

"Whether you had anything to do with it or not—"

"I didn't—"

"Relax. What I meant was, the world wasn't sure—my point being that it should be an effective deterrent, y'know, if anyone thinks they can rip us off."

Jack's voice was a near whisper, his eyes dark, his expression tight. He was serious. Dead serious.

"What the hell, Jack? I don't think a deterrent, as you call it, is necessary—"

"Oh yeah, it is, Buck. I'm the chief executive officer here. I work the analysts, massage the investors, and watch the numbers—that's my role while you're out grabbing the glory.

"Treasure hunting's a ruthless business, and our backers worry about us pissing money away on bullshit long shots. If the innuendo of this situation helped to prevent that, then it served some purpose."

He held up both hands. "Sure, I wish you hadn't gone through it, and we've been pounded in the market, but now that you're back, let's hope we get a higher percentage of quality data."

I left Jack's office shaking my head. If he thought my being accused of murder was good—

Papers went flying when I collided with someone at the corner of the hall.

"Damn—Buck? Is that you?"

It was Ron Zilke, e-Antiquity's chief financial officer. I'd forgotten how short he was, and his bald head glistened with perspiration as he gathered up his papers. "Welcome back, man. What a shit show that must have been."

His eyes darted from mine to his stack of papers, then down the hall toward Jack's office.

I nodded toward the board room. "How's the accounting review going?"

"You mean the audit?" His eyes were wide. He grunted loudly. "Fantastic. If you like colonoscopies, that is." He clutched his papers. "Gotta see Jack right now, but welcome back, kid. Hope you're ready to get to work."

He rushed down the hall to Jack's office and, once inside, closed the door behind him.
Audit?

18

"SURPRISE!" A HALF DOZEN OF OUR SUPPORT TEAM HAD gathered with a cake and balloons in the kitchen, which was on the way to my office on the opposite corner from Jack's. Hugs and congratulations came from the ladies, most of them in their mid-thirties, and I fielded a couple of high-fives from the guys on our logistics team.

"We wanted champagne to celebrate your wedding," one of the office assistants said.

"Or rum, to commemorate your release from Tortola," said Tommy, the youngest member of the logistics team.

Everyone laughed.

"Yeah, well, thanks for the sentiment on both fronts. I'm not sure which one I'm happier about." Antsy to get back to my office for the first time in ages, I didn't linger, just made sure first that they knew how much I appreciated the welcome.

Inside my office, I closed the door and just stood there, turning slowly around the room, taking in the many photographs on the walls…wait—something new. A framed copy of the *Wall Street Journal* article with me on the cover and the bold headline KING BUCK hung in the center of the wall. A faded ribbon taped to the frame dangled from the bottom. I scanned the article and stopped on the quote from Jack Dodson: "We estimate the value of the Guatemala antiquities to be in excess of five hundred mill…"

I distinctly remembered telling Jack that Scarlet and I, along with the people from the university, estimated the value at closer to *one* hundred fifty million. Typical for him, inflating values to excite investors.

All my other pictures were from different excavations, mostly me holding up some relic or jewels. Of all the pictures taken in the field, Scarlet was featured in at least half. We'd been quite a team. I owed her my freedom, but I missed her in many ways, not least of which were her analytical abilities, her knack of spinning things to our—*my*—benefit, her company and friendship, and yes, our special relationship while out in the field.

But meeting Heather had changed all that overnight. My wife's being the international supermodel knocked my socks off—not to mention her beauty and sex drive.

I shrugged those thoughts aside and removed my framed University of Virginia diploma from the wall to check the contents of my safe. Nobody had the combination but me, and I'd never worried about writing it down because I'd programmed it to be my birthday, along with those of my parents and brother. It popped right open to reveal the thick binder of maps, letters, and clues to other treasures I'd spent the past four years collecting. Behind the binder was the envelope holding my emergency twenty thousand dollars in cash.

I opened the folder and scanned each archival sleeve. Every continent was represented. The contents had been acquired in myriad ways, including private auctions, estate sales, brokers, and historic archives on loan from universities or other collectors. Based on our successes to date, the value of the collective treasures could amount to billions of dollars.

I stopped on the sleeve for Mexico. Cody was there now, according to Jack, searching for details of additional Mayan activity near Cozumel. We'd discussed this as a logical opportunity in the height of the excitement over the Guatemala find, but I'd never categorically decided that it would be the next effort. Jack had never made a decision like that without me. How much of a voice had Cody had in suggesting it? My role was to lead the discovery and archeological efforts, and just as Jack kept me out of the investor meetings, I considered this my turf.

I'd already discussed with Heather the importance of my getting back into the field, and given all the different fashion weeks and the release of the various designers' new catalogues, we knew it could be a busy six months. I closed the binder.

The sooner I repeated our success in the field, the sooner I could come home. I picked up my phone and pressed zero.

"Hi, Buck. How can I help you?"

"Sadie, can you arrange for Net Jets to pick me up at Dulles in the morning? I need to be in Mexico City tomorrow afternoon."

"Not wasting any time, are you?" she said.

I chuckled. "My father taught me that there's no better time to produce your next success than just after your last one. Too much time has passed already, and I need to get moving."

"You got it."

"One other thing? Get me the information on where Cody's staying and let him know I'm on my way."

19

I SPENT THE NEXT TWO WEEKS WITH CODY IN MEXICO CITY. I was surprised to find television cameras and journalists camped out there to see me. Cody's research had failed to yield anything new, and the curator of the archives was discouraged—and concerned about the attention my presence was causing. I was impatient. Cody and I agreed that he'd stay and I'd double-down by opening another research site. Unfortunately, though, my leaving Mexico to Cody was misperceived, and the headline in *La Prensa*, translated, read KING BUCK STRIKES OUT IN MEXICO CITY.

Nothing was more irritating than unidentified sources that turned our efforts into wild-goose chases. We always learned something of value in these archival deep dives, even if it meant there was nothing new on file. Cody continued the search, and the archives curator was relieved that the spectacle following me had dissipated with my departure, but this did nothing to discourage bad press.

Jack called me at the hotel. "The story in *La Prensa* was a kick in the butt, Buck. Can't you pull some rabbit out of your ass to keep the investors off mine?"

"A second front of research elsewhere is a better story than a concentrated effort on a case that's had minimal results. I'm headed to Normandy to dive the English Channel off Cherbourg to search for a Roman ship carrying plunder from ancient England." I omitted to mention that Heather was in nearby Mont St. Michel on assignment.

"Did Scarlet work on that? Is it solid?"

"Would I be going there if it weren't solid?"

The long flight was a blur as I worked the phones non-stop, organizing an impromptu team of French divers and academic experts in Roman history. By Iceland I was comfortable that I had a competent team, and I sat back to appreciate the beauty of rocketing across the Atlantic aboard the Gulfstream jet. I reclined my seat, sipped champagne, and called Heather.

"Bonsoir, chérie," I said.

"Buck! I'm dying here in this tiny town. I miss my big strong man."

"Can you meet me for breakfast at the Château La Chenevière just north of Caen?"

Her quick intake of breath followed by a squeal made me laugh.

"I'll take that as a yes."

I toasted her with a glass of Veuve Clicquot, then slept a couple of hours. When we landed, I was escorted through Customs and whisked off in a limo to my hotel, a classic French chateau in a bucolic wooded setting.

"Madame Reilly has already checked in, monsieur," the receptionist said.

Heather opened the door before I knocked. She pulled me inside—she was naked—and flung me toward the bed. I bounced, already laughing, and she was on top of me, pressing her lips against mine while pulling at my shirt with one hand and undoing my belt with the other.

"When did you get here?" I said.

"I couldn't sleep—I came last night—and I came just waiting for you."

I kicked my shoes off as she pulled my pants down, then my socks, and made her way back up my body—very slowly. By the time her face was back to mine I spun her over and lowered myself onto her. We fit like a soft hand in a silk glove—when she yelped, I lost myself and collapsed on top her, both our bodies slick with sweat.

Once her breathing settled, she spoke first. "You said something about breakfast?"

We spent the day in the room, making a dedicated effort to flatten out the lumpy mattress. By nightfall, in big trouble with the director of her shoot, Heather skedaddled back to Mont St. Michel, leaving me to coordinate the half-dozen men, dive gear, and trawler I'd arranged to take us to the coordinates that Scarlet had pieced together from multiple sources, landmarks, and the account of a lone survivor written before his execution for losing the vessel.

Ten-foot waves, a driving north wind, and rain slapped our ship around the English Channel, but the divers were professionals, and we blindly scoured the area a quarter-mile off the coast where I hoped to find the remains of the Roman vessel, or at least the metallic signature of the treasures they'd stolen from England. After six days, my contract with the crew and vessel had run out, and while I could have doubled down, in my gut I felt we were nowhere near finding anything other than garbage and a sunken fishing boat.

Translated, the headline in *Le Monde* meant, KING BUCK LOSING HIS TOUCH? The story went on to note that e-Antiquity had found nothing off Cherbourg.

That condemnation scalded me. Just a year ago, nobody would've paid attention to my activities, even if I'd been digging up the Champs Élysées in front of the Arc de Triomphe. But now I was hounded by news media that seemed as enamored by my failures as they'd been by my successes.

Back at the Château La Chenevière, my hopes to again find Heather in the room were dashed by darkness and a red blinking light on the phone. The recording told the story: "I'm sorry, darling, but I already set the shoot back a day, and Chanel is in a hurry to complete their campaign before the show starts in Paris next week. Hope you found some new treasure! Have a safe trip home. Kisses kisses."

Damn.

At least Jack didn't know where I was, but his emails and voicemails had become more desperate. The latest: "I've done my part and have great investors and operating capital. You need to find something of value or it'll all fall apart." Next, I heard him bear down hard. "Be the king they think you are."

"Thanks, Jack."

I spent the rest of that evening in the room's red leather chair combing through my travel copy of the binder of potential prospects I'd brought from my wall safe at the office. I yawned. The room was dead silent except for a giggle through the wall—a female giggle. I leaned my head back for just a moment. When I awoke in the chair at 1:35 a.m. to find the binder open to Seville, Spain, I decided to let fate carry me there. As I crawled under the thick down comforter into the cold bed, it wasn't Heather but Scarlet I was missing—as a strategist to help me deduce which targets were meaningful opportunities. My powers of deduction were rusty. A night's tossing and turning ultimately drove me to abandon the bed at dawn.

By the time room service arrived with the breakfast I'd ordered the night before, I was on my way out the door with my bag in hand.

"Do you need a driver, monsieur Reilly?" the receptionist said.

"*Oui, à l'aéroport rapidement, s'il vous plaît.*"

Then on my phone to the pilot: "Crank her up, captain. We're going to San Pablo Airport in Seville, Spain."

In the midst of this spontaneous, or at least poorly planned, European trip, I remembered a report I'd come across a couple years before that originated from Seville's Archeology Museum about missing amphorae full of bronze and silver coins dating back to the late third and early fourth centuries.

The research was based on records from the Roman army of a trial related to the missing payroll for five hundred men camped near the town of Tomares. The article noted that the ancient thieves had reportedly stolen a convoy carrying some twenty jars of currency, and all but two guards had been murdered. During the ensuing inquisition, the two survivors' stories fell apart, yet neither would reveal the location of the payroll, so both had been hanged. The conclusion had been that the jars must be somewhere close to where the other guards had been murdered, since the jars and their contents were too heavy for the pair of men to carry far. In view of the style and size of the amphorae common for the period, they'd have weighed approximately a hundred pounds each, for a combined total of more than two thousand pounds of rare Roman coins.

Ana Navanno of the Archeology Museum had written

the article, and I had an appointment with her at 11:00 a.m.

During the flight I'd had my research team in Virginia email me a presentation on e-Antiquity and the El Mirador find, closing with the new exhibition being prepared at the National Museum of Archeology and Ethnology in Guatemala City.

A limo took me west into Seville. We traveled down the Avenida de Kansas City to a circle at the end, where we turned onto a road whose name caused my mouth to fall open. Calle El Mirador. If that wasn't a good sign, I had no idea what would be.

We passed first through a congested commercial district and then by the stunning Moorish architecture of the University of Seville, founded just nine years after Columbus arrived in America. We drove until we reached the lush green oasis of Parque de Maria Luisa, site of the famous museum El Prado—I laughed out loud—on the Plaza de América.

A reflecting pool held a dappled mirror image of the museum behind it, so ornate and lavish it looked more like a Disney theme park. A docent directed me up a staircase and into a reception area where I was asked to wait in a small conference room. My suit was rumpled, and, given the past several weeks, I hoped it didn't smell worse than it looked. By the time Ms. Navanno arrived I had my laptop powered up and the presentation on cue in case the opportunity arose.

"Ah, Mr. Reilly, such a pleasure!"

She was a short, squat woman with a bright burgundy birthmark in the shape of Italy on her cheek. Her dull gray dress belted with a cord of the same color gave her the appearance of a monk, but her smile was broad and welcoming.

We chatted briefly about El Mirador, and she nodded with interest at the prospect of the presentation. Her area of specialty centered on Europe, primarily during the Roman Empire, but the Serpent King and the Mayan—*the Reilly*—Codex were such amazing finds that she was engrossed in each image, map, and detail of how I finally discovered the crypt by overlaying the constellation Orion and specific stars on correspondingly placed landmarks in the ancient city.

"Bravo, Mr. Reilly," she said when I finished.

"Please, call me Buck." I waited for her nod then changed the subject. "Now, I'm fascinated by a paper of yours I read a couple years ago—"

"*La nómina de pago*—the missing Roman Army payroll?"

"Exactly. Our firm would be interested in teaming with the museum, under very friendly terms for Spain, to help you search for these historically significant antiquities."

Her head bobbed enthusiastically. "I'd guessed you might propose this, so I spoke to my director after you requested this meeting. We'd certainly be interested in discussing this, once we have proper authorization from the ministry." When she smiled, the boot of Italy kicked forward on her cheek.

Her response wasn't a surprise, so I turned on my brightest smile and glanced back at the image of the Serpent King's crypt before we'd emptied it.

"Of course, but it would be helpful to review your data before exercising the ministry. How long is their typical process when considering these opportunities?"

She grimaced, her lips as tight as a walnut.

"It can take up to two years to get approved, if at all." She shook her head. "Most requests are denied, but—"

"During that time, you see, our team of archeologists could be evaluating your data and ancient maps—"

"I'm sorry, Mr. Reilly—Buck—but we're strictly prohibited from sharing research with industry, especially someone as noteworthy as yourself, before we have proper authorization."

My heart sank.

"I will, however, request that they expedite the normal collaboration application process, and I'd guess that by this time next year we may have permission to proceed." Her smile revealed crooked teeth the same color as her dress.

When I puffed out a loud breath her eyebrows went up. She *was* trying to help, and she *was* interested, but these things took time. Bureaucracy always does. I'd been so anxious to hit the ground running, I'd hoped that my success in Guatemala would cut through the typical red tape. It was efforts like these that Scarlet had undertaken for us, often a year ahead of the fieldwork. Hell, it had taken her eighteen months to get permission from the Guatemalan government for our El Mirador excavation.

I had to get her back, else we'd fall even further behind!

After Ana Navanno and I spoke of next steps, she agreed to commence discussions, through her director, who was "disappointed not to be here today," but he was in Barcelona at a conference. I thanked her, and to my surprise, she leaned forward and hugged me, in appreciation of e-Antiquity's desire to work with the museum.

On the way back to the airport, I called Jack.

"We have a verbal commitment to proceed in Seville, subject to the ministry's approval."

He groaned. "That'll take forever."

"We're loading up the pipeline—"

"That won't cut it. What else did Scarlet have underway before she quit?"

A damned good question. I hadn't spoken to her about business for more than a year, and my time off, followed by the endless incarceration, had left a cold trail. "Mostly the Mexican work Cody's now pursuing—"

"Shit!"

"I'm on my way home—"

"Fly commercial."

That caught me off guard. Jack had never been one to count pennies.

"The jet's here in Seville, Jack."

A cold silence followed.

"I'll see you soon," I said.

The line went dead.

The previous month's auditors in our office came to mind. Time to find out what the hell was going on.

But first things first.

I squeezed the satellite phone so tight I was afraid it would crack, until I heard her voice.

"Greetings from Europe."

"Buck? Is that you?"

"We need you back, Scarlet. *I* need you back."

A brief silence followed. "Are you on your way home from France?"

I tilted my head back. "Are you bored yet? You can't be having as much fun as we had—"

"I'm not bored, don't worry about that." She cleared her throat. "I can't come back, Buck. Not now, probably not ever."

My stomach dropped. Damn.

"And please don't press me, I don't want to talk about it." She hesitated. "But I do miss being in the field, e-Antiquity, and you—"

"So why—"

"I'm not coming back. I can't. Just understand that, okay?"

The limo pulled into the private aviation area of the airport and drove all the way up to the gleaming Gulfstream jet on the tarmac. I sat frozen in the back of the car, not wanting to hang up.

"And I need to get off the phone now—"

"Scarlet, wait! Please! just let me thank you for everything, for our success, for helping get me out of Tortola—"

"I did that as much for me as you."

And with that, the connection went dead.

SECTION 3

LIFE IN THE FAST LANE

20

OUR NEW HOME IN GREAT FALLS WAS EMPTY OF EVERYTHING but furniture and me. No pets, no children, no wife. All the years of returning home from international trips to an empty condo had been like an old wound that had healed over in the time since I'd met Heather. Or so I thought. Our six months of constant companionship had been interrupted by my incarceration on Tortola, followed by our collective travel demands.

I headed to the office.

I was transcribing my written notes from Mexico, France, and Spain when Jack walked in.

"I'm taking the ball and calling an audible, Buck," he said. "The wheels are in motion."

"Wheels? Audible?"

"Plan B." He quirked an eyebrow. "Actually, Plan SB."

His rueful grin brought back memories of a Jack I hadn't seen in a long time. "Okay, I'll bite, what's Plan SB?"

"St. Barths."

It only took two weeks to convince our largest investors and several others whom Jack had been courting to meet us in Miami, where a chartered yacht waited. At 140 feet, the Nomad was the largest yacht available in the hemisphere, with a crew of twenty-two ready to cater to our every need. We were scheduled to arrive in St. Barths on December 23rd.

Jack's premise for the trip was simple—a thank-you for those who had contributed to the amazing success of e-Antiquity so far, and an opportunity for new blood to see and hear at first hand from the company executives and other satisfied investors. It promised to be a memorable voyage.

"Bottom line," Jack had said, "I need to raise capital, thanks to your lack of new discoveries. That lack has caused our stock price to flounder, compounded the renewal of our soon-to-expire hundred-million dollar credit line, and exacerbated lenders' concerns as to whether our investors might sell out."

"Ron told me we were getting audited. What's up with that?"

"We sell treasure, Buck. Stuff you find in third-world, rogue nations. We're not Procter and Gamble or General Electric. We can't always quantify our costs, and all the notoriety in Guatemala, your highness, actually increased the scrutiny of our books." Our eyes held. "Not to mention Tortola."

I winced.

"Frankly, given the nature of our boom-and-bust spike in revenues, it's not always easy to keep the books looking great, so do yourself a favor and leave that to me. Okay?"

He patted my shoulder.

Ron Zilke's sweat-soaked underarms and brittle laugh when I asked him to review our financial situation with me suggested Jack was far more concerned about our corporate health than he'd let on. Bigger companies were holding parties in Las Vegas, Texas, New York, or at private five-star retreats, replete with 70s or 80s rock bands, hookers, even drugs and cash gifts for their investors, so he felt we could get away with the boondoggle to the French West Indies.

Jack admired such former industry titans as WorldCom and Enron who'd been known for excessive entertainment. Our own e-Antiquity was much smaller, so he rationalized that a smaller group sailing the Caribbean would go unnoticed—never mind that it was going to cost a fortune. I loved St. Barths, which Heather had introduced me to before we were married, bringing me along on a swimsuit modeling gig, so if Jack thought it made financial sense, who was I to argue?

Since I'd returned from Europe Heather and I had only seen each other a couple of times, but we did manage a rendezvous in New York before my investor trip with Jack. She flew in from Europe, as I did from Washington, and met for dinner at Le Bernardin.

She was looking puzzled. "St. Barths with a group of investors—all men—for Christmas?"

"Jack's idea, and since you're scheduled to be back in Europe and said I couldn't come—"

"On a yacht?"

"I'd love for you to come, Heather. Can you reschedule your assignment?"

"No, I can't. I've done this event in Paris for three years in a row now—"

"With a French playboy billionaire—"

"He's nearly seventy, Buck."

"He's a billionaire, Heather. We both know you love money—"

"Excuse me? Mister Accused of Killing Someone Over Money in Tortola?"

I stormed out of the restaurant. Stood outside on the corner of 7th Avenue watching cars hurtle toward the lights of Times Square and waited for a text, or a call, or for Heather to walk outside to find me, but she never did. After thirty minutes I went back inside to find her finished with her appetizer and main course, and both of mine sitting there cold.

"I'm ready to leave," she said.

She never apologized, backed down, or warmed up back at the hotel either. The next day she left early for her assignment and I returned to Virginia.

Happy freaking holidays.

We'd only managed one quick conversation after she arrived in Paris, and even though I'd asked to schedule calls, she'd been noncommittal. My phone messages and emails went unanswered. I wished I could jet off to see her in Paris, but I knew Jack was right—all my months of screwing off had put the company in a hole that I now had to dig us out of. Heather and I would be reunited after New Year's, at a location to be determined.

White water peeled off the sleek silver bow of the Nomad as we carved an arcing path around St. Maarten toward the silhouette of St. Barths. Our guests were either successful businessmen or came from old moneyed families, and with few exceptions they liked to start drinking early and continue through the day. None seemed to mind leaving families behind for the holidays.

The morning of our second day at sea, though, the group was getting restless.

"What is this," Jacob Harrison said, "some kind of gay cruise?" He was a venture capitalist from New York whom Jack had been cultivating.

Jack smiled. "We have a week on St. Barths, Jacob. You won't be disappointed."

A horn sounded, and the ship shifted course subtly to port.

One of the mates hurried by and up to the bridge. I followed after him—past Andrew Reinach, a construction mogul from Boston who'd been glued to his phone the entire day. The captain was on the radio and tapping his fingers rapidly on the console. The mate who'd run past me now peered through binoculars ahead of the yacht.

"What's going on?" I said.

"Big ship backing out of Gustavia harbor."

"Is that a problem?"

He glanced at the captain, then me. "It's Muammar Qaddafi. He's been denied entry by the St. Barths government. His security staff is armed and angry. We need to keep our distance."

I walked forward and saw a huge gray ship throwing out a broad wake as it backed out at a speed faster than appropriate. Moored and anchored boats of all sizes rocked at dangerous angles. Armed men could be seen on each deck of the yacht.

Crap.

I walked back onto the bridge. The captain glanced up at me, his mouth a tight line. "Son-of-a-bitch tried to steal our mooring spot."

The captain waited until Qaddafi's yacht was out of the way, then proceeded at a prudent speed into the harbor where boats were still rocking on the wake of the Libyan dictator's ship. The speed and accuracy with which the captain backed the massive yacht into the tight slip between two lesser but still massive yachts was impressive. The moment the purr of our engines died away, cheering sounded from the afterdeck.

Outside, I found our guests standing at the rail, waving to a group of fifteen— no, twenty—beautiful women in bikinis or skimpy dresses waiting for the gangplank to be lowered so they could come aboard. Jack slapped Jacob Harrison on the back.

"Still think it's a gay cruise?"

From the back of the group I watched, feeling no compulsion to rush into the fray as the ladies stepped onto the deck, taking glasses of champagne from trays held by our multi-purpose crew. Amazing how being a newlywed had changed my priorities. Jack had been married eight years, had two young children, and in the past had said he lived vicariously through me. It only took a glance to realize he was planning to bust loose here.

Not me. The women who'd come aboard were some of the most beautiful I'd ever seen, but none was Heather Drake-Reilly.

21

The week was a blur of parties, fancy dinners, diving, hiking, sailing, dancing, and decadence. The final day was upon us and included a concert we'd organized on the quay next to the yacht basin. We mingled with celebrities, several of them here with mega-investor Bernie Madoff from New York, whom Jack had invited to hang out on our yacht since Madoff handled his money. Bob Fink, a partner at Lehmann Brothers, was cradling a double magnum of Dom Perignon as if it were a toddler, pouring mouthfuls into every blonde woman he passed.

"Blondes have more damn fun!" he shouted every time one swallowed a slug.

A loud guitar riff sounded, and from my vantage point on the back deck I saw Dave Grohl from the Foo Fighters swinging his long hair in a flurry, locked into a guitar duel with Joe Walsh as a few of the Eagles belted out "Hotel California."

The energy of St. Barths, the concentration of millionaires, billionaires, movie stars, models, musicians, yachts, booze, drugs, and fluff money was unlike any place I'd ever seen. Impromptu concerts had been occurring for days here on the quay, all part of the build-up to what had been an epic holiday on the island. One musician, singer-songwriter Keith Sykes, was now seated on one of our yacht's couches with me. Across from us was Harry Greenbaum, an Englishman who was our largest investor. He'd chosen to skip the lunacy aboard the yacht and fly to St. Barths separately to stay in a private villa. Also in our circle was Marius Stakelborough, owner of Le Select, the central watering hole and cheeseburger emporium in Gustavia, and Bruno Magras, president of St. Barths. Our group wasn't drinking except for Keith, who was nursing a bottle of champagne. As for me, numb to the partying, semi-clad women, passed-out investors, and commitment ceremonies that Jack presided over on a daily basis, I wondered if this was how battle fatigue felt.

Harry Greenbaum watched some of the other investors at the table behind us, including a Merrill Lynch partner and an up-and-comer from Bear Stearns, plus some other asshole know-it all from Lehmann Brothers, gambling, drinking Cuban rum, smoking cigars, and boasting of financial conquests. A loud belch from one of the gamblers made Harry grimace and turn his attention back to us. Keith was suddenly dozing, his head on Marius's shoulder, but the bar owner didn't bat an eye.

A pang of guilt passed through me—Jack had done the heavy lifting all week. He'd told me during a sober moment that commitments from the investors so far had exceeded fifty million dollars.

"Mark my words, gentlemen," Harry said, "this fantasy of an economy will soon come tumbling down."

Bruno nodded.

"Remember," I said, "the value of antiquities only goes up."

Harry went on. "We're on the last legs of what's been an amazing run-up since Congress gave financial institutions permission to comingle funds between investment banks and regular banks. Combine that with unregulated derivatives, low interest rates—"

Another burp sounded from the Lehmann partner, who stood up, bent over the rail, and retched.

"As for the global economy," Harry said, "it's poised for calamity."

"The real-estate boom here has been meteoric," Bruno said. "Protection against overdevelopment inflated villa values." He sipped at a sparkling water. "People who would not normally have access to capital are buying second homes here with American mortgages that require no money down."

"Keep your powder dry, gentlemen," Harry said. "There will be an unprecedented buying opportunity ahead."

"How many companies do you own, Harry?" Marius said.

"At last count, twenty-seven." He popped a brie-covered cracker in his mouth, then dabbed the corners of his lips with a white cloth napkin. "I'm in the process of merging a few and disposing of others to prepare for what I expect to be a golden opportunity when the bubble bursts."

I sipped a warm beer. "Jack's convinced there'll only be a mild market correction."

Harry frowned. "Optimistic of him." He leaned forward. "Be careful, young man. As I'm advising all the executives in companies where I've invested, keep a close eye on your capital. If the market does move decidedly in the wrong direction, cash will be king, and paupers will starve."

A quiet moment settled over our group until Marius spoke.

"Maybe King Buck here will find El Dorado as an encore to his Mayan discovery."

I could have kissed him for changing the subject.

The crowd roared below us, where Jack and several guests were locked arm-in-arm with French, American, and Russian women, high-kicking to the music—one of the older men fell backwards with an over-zealous kick and brought half the line tumbling down on top of him, to an explosion of laughter.

Harry shot me a look. "No need to babysit us, Buck."

I shook my head. "I'm married to the most beautiful woman in the world, guys. My rambunctious days are over."

"Beauty is as beauty does, Buck," he said. "Never forget that."

Keith, back awake, held up the bottle of champagne. "I've been married twenty-five years. Cheers to that—"

"Buck! Buck! Buck! Buck!"

Jack Dodson had begun leading his gang in a chorus, shouting my name from the deck below us, then suddenly raced up the stairs to burst into the salon.

"Let's go, Reilly!" He tumbled toward me, and his lop-sided grin and wild glassy eyes promised trouble. "Come on—you've been heartsick this entire trip! Time to celebrate *my* success, dammit!"

He grabbed my arm and pulled me off the couch, oblivious of the other guests around me. I stumbled after him down the steps into a bevy of female arms waiting for me like a catcher anticipating a fast ball.

"*Bonjour*, baby!" The tall brunette who'd caught me was laughing and immediately nuzzling my neck, as two other women swooped in from each side, pulling my shirt loose, then—rip!

Women caressed, hugged, and kissed my now bare neck, shoulders, and chest, to the sound of male cheering. Our wilder guests pumped their fists, cheered, and gyrated with women, while a photographer captured the bacchanalia. Jack directed the women and the photographer, slapping high-fives with everyone when the camera flashes blinded me—what the hell?

I covered my face and pulled free of the embrace of three young, wild-eyed, glistening women wearing nothing but butt floss and glitter. As they pulled at me, I struggled loose in a barrage of camera flashes. The photographer was gone by the time I extricated myself from the phalanx of flesh and came face-to-face with Jack.

"I did it!" He raised both palms beckoning me to slap them.

"Who was taking pictures?" I said.

"Seventy-five million in commitments!" He slapped his hands against mine.

"Where's that photographer?"

"Seventy-five fucking-million dollars—and that doesn't include Harry!"

"Jack! Who was taking pictures of me and those girls?"

He pumped his fists in the air to the retro disco music that blasted over the yacht's sound system. For a moment, his eyes focused, then he looked away. "Photographer? He's from *Pure Magazine*, a local lifestyle rag—seventy-five million, baby!"

Women enveloped him and he vanished amid breasts and willowy arms.

Son-of-a-bitch.

Jack had hit his goal. The beat of the music sucked me in, and soon I was guzzling shooters and partying with the best of them. Our last night was a marathon soirée, even by St. Barths standards, and the next day everyone limped away via chartered planes from St. Barth Commuter back to wives, families, and reality.

I hadn't spoken to Heather since I'd come to St. Barths. Jack's and my private jet hurtled over the Caribbean, and while he snored, I recalled Heather on the beach in the Virgin Islands, in bed in France, and then at Le Bernardin in New York. I couldn't get home soon enough. I just hoped she'd be there when I arrived.

22

"WHO GOES TO ST. BARTHS FOR CHRISTMAS?" HEATHER said. "With all those drunken assholes and whores?"

"I haven't been home for five minutes and this is the greeting I get?"

"Damn straight," she said.

"It was a massive boondoggle to raise money. Jack assembled some horny old bastards who—"

"Have you seen the entertainment magazines? You're sandwiched between two topless bitches—it was on the national news! They lambasted you for squandering investors' money like moronic playboys."

Heather was right, and the news about our equity-raising trip had been anything but generous. Yeah, we raised a ton of cash, but the bad news and resulting impact on the stock price countered those gains. The media had smeared unflattering pictures of me and several guests cavorting with scantily clad women all over the place. The photo of me squashed between champagne-wielding naked women in *Pure Magazine* became emblematic of the entire debacle.

"I didn't do anything wrong—"

"Bullshit."

"You have no reason to doubt me, Heather—"

"Ten million television viewers and *National Enquirer* readers disagree with you, and so do I. Do you know how that makes me look? I've built my reputation on a wholesome, healthy image of fucking purity!" She shook her fists at me.

I ducked.

"My agency had to dispatch a publicist to Paris for damage control. Everyone was consoling me—even Givenchy expressed concern! I'm the top model in the world—how does it make me look with my already tarnished husband half naked between Russian hookers?"

She threw her smaller Louis Vuitton handbag on the couch.

I bit my trembling lip, trying to conjure restraint, unsuccessfully, especially since I'd found a picture of Heather in the same gossip magazine I'd appeared in.

"So what about those pictures of you sitting on that French billionaire's lap then? Huh? Was that your publicist's idea of how to save your wholesome image?"

She turned away, but not before I saw the smirk on her face.

"What is he, seventy years old? And this was your third Christmas together?"

"Jean-Claude's... a dear friend—"

"I'm not the jealous type, Heather, but the gossip rags say there's more to it than a *dear friendship*. And you were supposed to be in Paris—why were you in Val-d'Isère skiing?"

"It was the Christmas holidays! My husband had ditched me for a bevy of bimbos, what was I supposed to do?"

"I asked you to join me. You had your annual trip with the French billionaire you wouldn't break. You think I wanted to be there with Jack and those jerk-offs?"

"Looks like you made the most of it."

Heather grabbed the small bag she'd thrown earlier and pulled a pack of cigarettes out and lit one.

"What the hell? When did you start smoking?"

"I smoke when I'm upset, which means I've been smoking a lot lately."

I waved my hand through the smoke she'd blown at me. "Well, don't do it in the house."

With that I grabbed my luggage, still by the front door after the taxi had dropped me—Heather had refused to pick me up at Dulles—and carried it upstairs. So much for the warm reunion I'd hoped for.

Inside our room I stopped abruptly and dropped my bags.

Heather's suitcases were by the door. I lifted one—full.

I stepped back in the hall. "What's this—"

HONK! HONK!

A car horn sounded from in front of the house.

"What's that?" I said.

"My ride. I'm leaving for Europe."

I hurried down the stairs three at a time. "Please, don't leave now. We need to—"

"We don't need to do anything."

She dodged my spread arms and stomped up the stairs, only to return a moment later dragging two jumbo suitcases behind her.

"How could I have been so stupid?" The curl of her eyebrow matched the scowl on her lips. "Falling for a treasure hunter!"

With that she stormed out the door.

23

FEBRUARY 2008

I CLOSED MY SUITCASE AND ZIPPED IT SHUT. MY CELL PHONE was on the bed, the speaker on.

"I'm on my way first thing in the morning," I said.

"About time we see some action," Jack said. "You and Cody hadn't found squat at the archives, so we're lucky that construction crew blundered onto what you couldn't."

"Thank God for the Cozumel runway extension," I said.

That had been yesterday.

The Mayans had been good to me. We were desperate for positive press and a bump in the stock, which for months had been bouncing along the bottom of our fifty-two-week low. It was up to me to prove that e-Antiquity and I were still relevant.

I ran a cold palm over my eyes.

"Listen, Buck, the analysts have been screaming ever since St. Barths—"

"I don't want to hear about it, Jack. Being away for Christmas and New Year's was a ridiculous idea. Heather still won't talk to me. Her silent treatment's the equivalent of the Cold War—"

"I told her you were a Boy Scout down there—"

"Yeah, well, those damn pictures on the yacht made her think otherwise."

"So, what, paybacks are hell?" Jack said.

The gossip rags had continued their speculation about Heather and the Parisian fashion icon, printing additional pictures of him with his face buried in her neck just last week. How had I been so stupid? Falling for a supermodel.

"I'm on Net Jets at seven a.m. out of Leesburg—"

"Why can't you fly commercial?"

"Don't bust my balls, Jack! We raised seventy-five million on that drunken boondoggle—"

"And the press crucified us, thanks to your pictures—"

" Pictures *you* got me into, and you know it. You, on the other hand were out of control."

"Most fun I've had in years."

"I was there, y'know."

"But the article that followed in the *Post* questioning whether we'd be the next Enron was a serious problem. Banks, investors, everyone's been up our asses. And the inquiries from the SEC have Ron Zilke sweating like a container of nitroglycerin—"

"That's your job—"

"Don't worry about what's my job, just do yours. And keep a low profile in Mexico."

Scarlet's warning from Guatemala had me biting my cuticles. I'd been on the top of the heap of history, or at least among historians, and she'd warned that my success and celebrity would only make me a target. Boy, had she been right.

Who was I kidding?

The truth was, Scarlet's departure had caused a research crevasse that I feared could never be bridged. It had taken a Mexican construction company to unearth antiquities Cody and I'd been unable to triangulate in on after months of effort.

Thanks to them, King Buck had new clothes.

24

Authorities from the University of Quintana Roo and the Mexican National Archives greeted my jet at the private aviation terminal in Cozumel.

"Señor Reilly." A short thin man in baggy gray slacks and khaki blazer waved to me.

A photographer stepped in front of him—Flash!

"Such an honor—I'm Carlos Acosta, from the university. We're under pressure from the government because the extraction has reduced airplane traffic to and from Cozumel. I fear we only have a day or two to prove the site is worth preserving."

"Understood, Señor Acosta. Our team will work fast."

"We'll take you straight to the site—much has already been, ah, discovered that we're anxious for you to review. And there's much more to find!"

Flash-Flash!

When his team stared up at me with doe eyes, my valve regulating self-worth opened wide and pumped pride into my veins.

I stood taller than I had in months when they shook my hand, bowed, called me Dr. Reilly, and grabbed my bags, chattering among, themselves in Spanish—a language I don't speak. They steered me toward Customs. Once expedited through, we walked outside to the arrivals area, and my greeters continued to bow and usher me forward like I was a Saudi prince.

King Buck was back.

The heat outside the terminal hit me like a bucket of warm piss. My handlers jogged to keep up with me as I walked quickly to the air-conditioned Toyota Land Cruiser. We weren't going far, and I was damned glad we weren't walking.

We entered a gated area past the terminal that led through brown desert scrub toward several large earthmoving vehicles, idle, unmanned, and baking in the sun. When we pulled up beside them I spied a large green iguana perched on the seat of a Caterpillar D8, front legs up on the dash of the huge yellow vehicle as if contemplating whether to run us over.

I marched ahead to the white tent where I found Cody Jacobson brushing dirt from a clay figurine.

"Hey, Buck." He put the relic down and we shook hands.

"What do we have here, Cody?"

He twisted his lips in an awkward pucker, then leaned closer. "Clay pots and a few statues like this one, so far." He glanced over at the university representatives, who were keeping their distance but watching us like expectant fathers during a C-section.

"They're hoping King Buck will pull a rabbit out of the rubble the local construction company pulverized before a security officer with a soft spot for his heritage stopped them."

My shoulders sagged.

Damn.

My eyes focused—blurred—then focused again on the small, plump, nude female figurine on the table. Ix-Chel, the Mayan fertility Goddess of the Moon. That made sense, since Cozumel and nearby Isla Mujeres had been destinations for women seeking to become pregnant back in the days of the Mayan empire. Ruins of temples devoted to Ix-Chel could be found all over the island, some dating back to the first millennium AD when the area had had a population of nearly ten thousand Mayans. Because the ruins of San Gervasio, the largest concentration of Mayan edifices, lay directly east of the airport, Cody and I had reasoned that this site could be an extension of it. In the Pre-Columbian era, it had been traditional for Mayan women to make a pilgrimage here at least once in their lives to fulfill certain vows and offer sacrifices.

Our speculation was that families would bring some of their most valuable possessions here as offerings, hoping it would bring them children, and we further postulated that the priests collected these valuables and stored them in a yet-to-be discovered location. That missing cache, if it existed, was what we were after now.

Cody rolled his eyes. I gave him a slight nod.

"Let's see if we can connect the dots on our theory."

Flash-Flash-Flash!

The photographer from the terminal shot pictures of Cody and me hovering over the figurine as if it were the Serpent King's personal pocket goddess.

"Follow me," Cody said.

He led me out of the tent to a series of shallow pits, in three of which laborers were lackadaisically sweeping at gravel with ordinary brooms. A couple of similar figurines stood erect beside each trench. The photographer was taking close-ups of each one when something else caught my eye. I stepped to my right, walked twenty feet, and stopped. Fists on hips, I bent down and stared at a pile of broken pottery I assumed had been collected in the wake of the construction.

Click-Click!

The photographer captured images of the clay chunks, then fell to his knees to shoot images of me from the ground up. I held my stare on the shattered figurines. Best case, if they'd been in the same condition as the one Cody was cleaning in the tent, would be a market value of maybe five thousand dollars each. I crossed my arms and shook my head. Jack would not be happy.

"Reilly!"

A familiar Southern accent caused me to spin on my heel.

"Craig Dettra?" Shocked to see the archeologist from the Smithsonian here at our site, I twisted back to catch Cody's eye.

"Forgot to tell you. Jack hired Craig. Wanted extra horsepower."

His calloused hands grabbed at my arms and I mustered a smile as we half-hugged. His team from Washington appeared behind him—talk about bringing a sledgehammer to squash a mouse. We caught up as we returned to Cody's command tent. Craig had been on medical leave after contracting yellow fever in the wilds of Peru, and this was his first trip afterward.

"Guess we're both a little rusty," I said.

"Rusty, right." He winked at me.

Inside the tent we pored over the charts, aerial photographs, and every noted ruin on the island of Cozumel. The system I'd discovered in Guatemala of overlaying major temples with the star chart of Orion didn't work here, as there was nothing so significant that it could serve as a lynchpin. Santa Rita, a smaller set of ruins, lay between San Gervasio and the airport. Santa Pilar was to the northwest of the airport, Castillo Real was to the northeast, El Cedral was on the southern tip, and the largest town, San Miguel, was southwest of the airport.

I stared at the map for several minutes, closing out the voices around me, the mosquitoes circling my head, and the whine of jet airliners descending. Sweat trickled down my spine—it made me think of a straight line.

I took Cody's ruler and a carpenter's pencil and connected the sites in straight lines, seeking a pattern. The heaviest concentration was here on the northern end of the island, and the airport was directly between Santa Rita and Santa Pilar, the latter now a luxury beach resort. If anything of value had been found there during construction, it was never made public. In most cases, discoveries like that would be used to brand attractions for tourists, so I concluded nothing had been found. While both these previous sites were less important, they were known to be villages where priests had lived. One of our ancient maps showed a path that connected the two, just to the north of what was now the airport, which was maybe a hundred and fifty yards north of where we stood now. The area had remained as undeveloped scrubland.

I pointed to the spot on the map. "That's where I want to search."

A flurry of whispers in Spanish commenced behind me, followed by multiple clicks of the camera to capture my finger stabbed onto the map.

"Let's go."

25

WE FOLLOWED THE LINE OF OPEN EXCAVATION PITS TO THE north, which was in the same direction as the runway. Heat waves lifted off the ground and distorted the scrubby jungle ahead. The unusually pungent smell of our sweat-soaked laborers didn't help. A plane came right at us, its tires screeching when it touched down. The smell of burnt rubber blew past us in blue smoke. A few moments later another plane took off, and as it climbed over our heads, the heat and blast of jet wash knocked me off balance—I tripped into the last excavation pit—rolled onto my hip and came to rest sitting on my rear end.

Shit—wait! *What?*

A shiny black object protruded from the dirt on the north side of the shallow hole. I bent closer—

"You okay, Buck?" Cody said.

"Hand me a trowel," I said.

A few moments later I'd dug around the object, which turned out to be a chunk of black stone, obsidian, hewn into the shape of a dagger. It was roughly eight inches long, and the handle—I blew dirt off it and rubbed it against my shirt—contained chunks of seashells forming the likeness of a bird's head.

Everyone gathered in close to me. I handed the object to Carlos from the university.

"Would a priest carry something like this?"

He accepted it gingerly, using both hands. He turned it around, then held the handle in the manner it had been intended.

"Yes, a priest, or a *nacom*, the officials who performed sacrifices."

He squinted at my sudden smile.

"Where's the map?" I said.

The excavation pits were noted, and the one I'd stumbled into was about fifty yards south of the road we'd been digging our way toward.

"Get the gear, I want to check around this area," I said. "A knife used by *nacoms* would be stored in a location of importance. So would the sacrificial offerings made by women seeking fertility."

The university team burst into a staccato of Spanish. They nodded their heads and bumped into each other as they ran in separate directions to grab tools. Over the next several hours we doubled the pace of excavating with small tools, brushes, and the palms of our hands to slide dirt and pebbles aside. The photographer hunched over our backs and documented each new relic, including a wide variety of clay figurines, stone carvings, a few bones, and some shattered clay pots. A cadre of men and women followed after us, delicately handling each item, wrapping them in packing material, numbering them, and placing them in metal crates trailered behind our six Kawasaki four-wheelers. I was surprised when three of the drivers pulled out and headed back toward base camp, their carriers full of antiquities.

Until now, what we'd found was typical of the majority of Mayan excavation sites with the exception of El Mirador. Crude archeological relics, none of which would yield seven-figure values. We pressed ahead, the mosquitoes attacking with a kamikaze vengeance as the sunset sky blazed orange. My own body odor now matched that of the laborers, which I realized was the combination of perspiration with the soil here that produced a nose-curling stench.

Darkness fell, and given the government's threats to close the dig in favor of the flow of tourists, we erected lights and gas generators to illuminate our path deeper into the ancient crossroads so we could work through the night.

"Cody, you take a team of four men and move in that direction." I pointed twenty degrees to the northwest. "Carlos, you and the other men from the university dig in that direction." I indicated the northeast. "I'll keep these four men and press straight ahead."

Cody nodded, and after Carlos repeated my orders in Spanish, their teams gradually angled away from the trench we'd dug over the last day, now thirty yards long and five feet deep. I used the light of my phone to consult the maps and aerial photos to assess our course and my hopes of triangulating in on a mother lode, if one existed.

A sudden recollection from Guatemala raised goose bumps on my arms. It was from the morning Scarlet and I'd awakened in my tent—hungover as hell—and our maps had been scattered on the floor the night before. The random placement of research material, combined with the aerial photo, had sparked the alchemy that led to our great discovery.

Our discovery.

I jammed my trowel into the dirt and heard a clunk.

My mind zagged to question whether Heather had appeared in any other magazines perched on the Frenchman's lap. Had she done that to get back at me for what she believed I'd done in St. Barths? Or was there more to it?

CLUNK!

One of the men in my hole turned hard toward me. I stabbed the trowel into the loose dirt—fuck it—

CLUNK!

"Señor, that doesn't sound like rock," the man next to me said. The image of Heather's face melted into his wide eyes.

After I finished carefully sifting, scraping, blowing, and pushing dirt aside, a green rectangular shape—jade by the look of it, roughly eighteen inches long—took shape before me. After a few moments, I realized the only other sound was the steady drone of the generators and bugs slapping into the halide lights. Everyone else had stopped to watch me.

Thirty minutes later, I lifted the box out of the ground. It was eight inches deep—and heavy.

Carlos sank to his knees to help me support the box, then scrambled after me as I pivoted toward the light and lowered our find into the circle of illumination.

FLASH! FLASH! FLASH!

Using a horsehair paintbrush, I delicately swept the surface of the box to reveal an intricate series of carvings that continued all the way around it.

"Looks like an urn," Cody said. "Maybe it's the cremated ashes of royalty."

Nobody laughed.

It once had had some type of metal or fabric hinges, but they'd long ago rotted into the Mexican soil. I took hold of the lid, and everyone leaned in closer. It was heavy—stuck shut. I shook it and the top popped free.

I laid the jade top aside—

"*¡Mi madre!*"

The voices cascaded into a single cry that made me flinch before I'd lowered the lid onto the dirt—a bright glow emanated from inside the box.

Gold.

26

THE DISCOVERY OF GOLD BOUGHT US MORE TIME FROM THE government. After another week of excavation and the discovery of more containers of precious items, including additional small amounts of gold, silver, jewels, several jeweled carvings, and dozens of clay pots and figurines, I was recalled to Virginia by anxious pleas from e-Antiquity's chief financial officer.

Officials from the Mexican *Consejo de Arquelogia del Instituto Nacional de Anthropologie e Historia*, who'd appeared at the site the day after we found the jade box, provided assurance of e-Antiquity's right to twenty percent of the goods and surprised me with a written commitment from the *Instituto's* president, Pedro Francisco Sánchez, that a Charles Reilly III exhibit would be established at the National Museum to honor our discovery in Cozumel.

Though I was touched by the gesture, it wasn't enough to dig us out of our financial hole, and apparently sufficiently disappointing that Jack hadn't even returned my calls. The *Wall Street Journal* showed our stock price was down. It had been momentarily buoyed by the find in Cozumel, then resumed its decline when the Mexican government released numerous pictures of the Mayan artifacts, only a fraction of which were of high monetary value, and noted that e-Antiquity would be limited to twenty percent of the find.

"Jack, why aren't you returning my calls?" The satellite phone crackled as I left him another voicemail.

As my Net Jet G-IV rocketed at max speed toward Dulles airport, I pulled a trinket out of my pocket. Inspired by the breakthrough in Cozumel, I'd spirited away a simple yet exotic fertility carving of a nude woman, clearly pregnant, as a gift for Heather. The entire experience had planted a wishful seed in my heart, which the pocket goddess had germinated into a hand-wringing fantasy to suggest to Heather.

What if we had a baby?

Tunnel vision? Yes. Wishful thinking? No doubt.

But I intended to suggest that we have a baby.

If she'd only answer her phone.

Heather's cell mailbox was full, and concern for her safety whirled in my stomach. I left an urgent message at her agency that they call me ASAP. Social media had little on me and nothing on Heather. For her to be low key on Twitter and Facebook was beyond odd.

When we landed at Dulles, I found no messages on my cell phone—nothing from Jack—and worse, nothing from Heather, either. The thirty-minute limo ride back to Great Falls was excruciatingly slow, and of course I found our house pitch-dark amidst the mature oaks, poplars, and hickory trees.

Inside, everything was as I'd left it. My note to Heather was still on the kitchen counter, partially buried under decomposed roses whose stems had siphoned putrid water from the Waterford vase onto the handwritten plea for reconciliation, obscuring the ink into fuzzy organic shapes that blended into the mold spores that had overtaken the page.

I stared at the note, unable to read the words but remembering having written: "Heather, I'm sorry. Can we have dinner and talk? Buck."

I leaned against the counter, my eyes fixed on the decay before me, not unlike the many relics I'd excavated from around the globe. Knowing she hadn't read the note hurt. Nothing I could think of had ever caused such anguish as the radio silence from Heather.

The answering machine!

I rushed to my study next to the kitchen—pictures of Heather and me, together and alone, stared down as I listened to all eight messages. I slumped into the chair.

Three from my father, two from my mother, two from Ron Zilke, and one from someone named Johnson from the Securities and Exchange Commission.

"Where are you son?" Dad x 3.

"Honey, call me the minute you return, I have news," Mom x 2.

"Buck, we have issues. Get your ass back here," Zilke, x 2. Our CFO had never spoken to me in that tone before.

Finally. "Mr. Reilly, we need to speak with you as soon as possible about e-Antiquity." Johnson from the SEC.

What the hell was going on?

And where the hell was my wife?

27

Jack hadn't returned my calls, and the stock was holding at nineteen, its lowest point since the IPO. The fifty-two-week high had been sixty-four.

I posted a couple pictures of the jade box and a few of the more impressive jeweled figurines and pieces of gold from Cozumel. Retweets and likes mounted quickly, along with a couple of too-little-too-late obnoxious messages that had my index finger hovering above my keyboard, but I pulled it back. Between Mexico, France, Spain, St. Barths, and back to Mexico, I'd been away so long I didn't know what reality was any more. It was time to find out.

I waited until late morning to return to the office. Tempted to return the call from Johnson at the SEC during my ride, I drove faster instead. Better to assess the situation first.

What I found at our luxury office made my jaw drop.

Paper was strewn all over the floor. Sadie was missing from the front desk, where mail was piled high. Music blasted from somewhere, and as I trudged down the hall toward the sound, I passed empty office after empty office—

some abandoned, others showing signs of having been hastily packed up and cleared out.

My inner core was numb as I marched toward the music—Led Zeppelin—"Stairway to Heaven."

Starky, our head of security, stuck his head out of his office, his eyes narrowing when our gazes met.

"What's going on, Starky? Where's the music coming from?"

He pointed down the hall and disappeared back into his office. At the end of the hall was the accounting department, which was littered with columns of paper stacked like corpses destined for the crematory. Ron Zilke was hidden behind twin towers of paper piled high on his desk, "Stairway" had ended and changed to "Misty Mountain Hop," and Robert Plant's shriek matched that of my inner voice with the volume maxed out.

"Zilke!"

I could see the top of his head bobbing around, but he didn't look up. I stepped forward and slapped the top of one of the paper stacks.

"Hey!"

He flew back in his chair—eyes wide—hands thrown up as if I were holding a gun. He was unshaven.

His fear morphed into a lip-curled stare.

Plant wailed about looking at yourself and whether you liked what you saw—Zilke slapped at the CD player—the room fell deathly quiet.

"Well, well, well, look who's back. King Buck." He shook his head. "I hope you brought a suitcase full of gold, 'cause we need it."

"Where is everybody?"

"Want some Scotch?" I noticed a bottle and a half-full rocks glass on his desk.

He didn't blink when he saw me check my watch. "Little early—"

"No, my friend, it's too late. *Way* too late." He emptied the glass, neat.

"What the hell's going on around here?"

"Trouble, and lots of it." He stared around him at the piles of paper. I noticed an official-looking stamp on one of them and leaned closer.

"SECURITIES AND EXCHANGE COMMISSION - DO NOT REMOVE." The stamp mark was in red ink. I fanned through the pile to find that each page had the same marking.

I swallowed, hard.

"Where's Jack?" I said.

Zilke rubbed his face with his palm, the rasp like a pepper grinder.

"Sit down."

I moved the chair from the front of his desk to the side so I could see him. The room felt tiny because there were so many stacks of paper, all with the SEC stamp.

He followed my gaze. "Have you spoken to them yet?"

"No, but there was a message from a guy named Johnson."

Zilke nodded. "That's the guy leading the investigation."

"*What fucking investigation?*"

Over the next hour Zilke took me through e-Antiquity's books, including our hundred-million-dollar credit line syndicated from fifteen banks that would expire in sixty-eight days. The renewal was not going well.

"Our four-hundred-million term loan matures in ninety-eight days, too." Zilke stared at me with gravedigger's eyes. "There are still more loans, but that's the big one."

"How much product do we still have in inventory?"

"Not nearly enough."

"What about revenue?"

He opened to the last 10-K and showed me that we had one hundred twenty million dollars of income in our public figures.

"Jack liked to exaggerate those, Buck. His philosophy has been to project revenue based on wishful thinking."

"But you're the chief financial officer, Ron. Why'd you let—"

"Don't even go there. Where were you for all of this?"

"Where was I? Out in shit holes around the world finding product—where do you think the cash and inventory came from?"

"You're the president of the goddamn company! Are you saying the CEO didn't keep you in the loop?"

"I did the archeology and Jack did the banking. That was our deal. Hell, he's dreamed of being a CEO since high school."

"Because he wanted the glory, but then you got all the press, *King Buck*—"

"What's that supposed to mean?"

Zilke pursed his lips, squinted, and leaned forward. "Jack used to describe you as the brawn to his brains, until you proved that differently with your discoveries. It changed him. Not long ago he said he'd turned into nothing more than an accountant."

"Jack hates accountants."

"Tell me about it."

"Jack's ego aside, how could our expenses have been so much greater than our income?"

The walls of the small office were closing in on me. I could smell Zilke's perspiration, or was it my own?

"Do you know how much that Guatemalan trip cost? And all the private freaking jets and first-class travel? Plus you being in jail and off-line for six months with no new discoveries killed us. And St. Barth's on a private yacht, for God's sake?"

My throat constricted. I couldn't swallow.

I'd been talking to him between two tall stacks of paper. I leaned forward and shoved the twin stacks off the sides of his desk—

WHOOSH! Several thousand pieces of paper crashed to the floor.

Zilke's eyebrows shot up and a slow smile spread over his face. With his eyes wide, he leaned forward and shoved the other stack of paper off his desk too.

WHOOSH!

Paper exploded all around me, and before it had even settled Ron was laughing hysterically. He spun around in his chair and kicked out at another pile, shearing off the top third of another—

WHOOSH!

He spun further, then pushed another pile toward the window—

"Ron! Stop it!"

He completed his circle until he was back facing me, and whether he'd laughed so hard it brought tears to his eyes, or he was just crying and laughing simultaneously, I wasn't sure.

"What the hell, man?"

"We're screwed, blued, and tattooed," he said, wiping his eyes.

I rocked forward and slapped my palm on the newly cleared corner of his desk—WHAP!

"Have you heard from Jack? Where is he?"

"Gone." He shook his head again. "Don't think he's coming back, either."

"Why d'you say that, Ron? What d'you know?"

"Because it's bad. I mean, *really* bad—"

"Tell me what the hell's happened."

"Jack made me lie. I didn't want to, but we lied to everyone. Investors, in our quarterly reports, annual report, you name it, man, I'm telling you. It was all fantasy on paper." A trail of snot dribbled from his right nostril.

I slowly sat back. "Lied? To everyone?"

"You too, Buck. Sorry. I never knew exactly what Jack had told you. He didn't want to discourage you out in the field, digging shit up, spending money like it was coming out your ass—he wanted you to. It was all a show. A spectacle, he called it."

"I've got to speak with him—"

"He ain't coming back, Buck."

"Why are you so sure?"

He groaned, got to his feet, and shifted his weight back and forth as he rocked in place.

"The money, man. The cash—our cash—our liquidity." He stopped rocking, tilted his fat, bald head back, and looked into my eyes. "It's gone. Cleaned out."

My ears suddenly felt as if they were stuffed with cotton, and everything went quiet. I caught myself leaning off the right side of the chair, scooted back into the seat, sat up straight. My heart clattered like a single cylinder, two-stroke engine with too much oil in the mix.

"How could he do that to me?"

Zilke poured more Scotch in his glass, then reached for the CD player. Led Zeppelin blared again, so loud it made my guts vibrate.

I lurched to my feet, swayed, and sucked in a deep breath. Out in the hallway I turned the corner and marched with increasing speed and urgency, feet pounding on the tight-pile carpet. At the end, I turned the corner to find Jack's secretary gone, her desk so neat that she couldn't be coming back. Jack's door was locked, and no sound came from inside.

I turned to find Starky standing in the corridor.

"Where is he?" I said.

"Mr. Dodson does not apprise me of his schedule."

"Unlock the door."

He gave me a long stare. "He's gone, Mr. Reilly."

I stepped back. "If your *boss* arrives—or calls—tell him his *partner* needs to talk."

Starky turned around, holding his pose as I brushed past him.

That guy had never liked me.

28

The balance of the day was filled with calls to board members, bankers, and analysts who covered our stock. I usually left those details to Jack and the finance team, but given the situation, I wanted to hear what they had to say at first hand.

"A lot of bad rumors out there, Buck," Scott Montgomery, one of our senior board members, said. "And the economy's crazy. How's it going with renewing the credit line? That's imperative."

He didn't mention the SEC. Jack must have not told the board. Hell, he hadn't even told me.

"Scary times. Ron and Jack are working closely with the banks. I'm searching for our next find, and we're confident all will be fine."

Lying to board members was new to me. I'd always been the wild-eyed optimist, talking about past, current, and future projects. That was my role. Jack handled all of the financial and operating company side. His team was huge, mine was Cody and Scarlet, and now I was down to half of that.

Would we be in this mess if she were still here? If I hadn't been wrongly jailed on Tortola? If I hadn't married Heather?

Next call was to Bank of America, our lead bank in the credit line. Given the tumultuous nature of the global financial markets, they had been under heavy pressure according to the news. Part of me was afraid to hear what they'd say, but I had to know what was going on.

"Charles Reilly, this is a first, you calling me," Robert Crider said.

"Just checking in with you, Bobby. I was meeting with Zilke this morning reviewing the status of the credit line—"

"Let me cut to the chase here, Charles. Since we purchased Countrywide Financial in January, we've had to circle the wagons."

"What're you saying, Bobby?"

"I'm saying to you what I've already told Jack—and what I've had to say to a lot of good clients—we're not likely to be renewing the line."

"But you're our lead bank—"

"And it's been a good relationship, but this global financial situation has us pretty damn worried. It's time to batten down the hatches."

"You spent *four billion* to buy Countrywide—"

"Uncle Sam forced our hand. It pretty much tapped us out."

After we ended the call I laid my head on my desk. How could this be happening? We'd made millions discovering amazing history that had been lost for centuries. How could it all unravel?

The next calls went to analysts who tracked and reported on e-Antiquity's stock. When it came to talking to analysts, it had always been a "What have you done for me this quarter?" kind of conversation, but today was worse.

Far worse.

"Nice job in Cozumel," one said, "but what you need is Guatemala times five." .

"Looks to us like you're liquidating."

"Stock's flat-lining, Buck. Not just e-Antiquity, but you're such a niche company, you have no industry cover."

In all I spoke to four analysts, every one of them willing to take my calls but none with anything good to say.

Still no word from Jack. His side of the business had fallen apart, and he'd left me to deal with it.

The sun was fading, and outside my window it was turning into a gray fall evening. Headlights passed in one direction on the Beltway, red lights on the other side of the median moved the other way.

To and fro, in and out, give and take, life and death.

Nobody had come right out and said it, but it was clear. We were dying—the financial equivalent of terminal cancer for e-Antiquity, and there was no kind of chemotherapy, CPR, transplant, or radiation that could produce a miracle cure.

Mementoes of accomplishment filled my office. Photos of successful campaigns, plaques from special honors, shovels, bones, clay figurines under glass, all the souvenirs from what most would measure as a lifelong career of thrills. I wasn't even thirty years old yet. I was too young to be done.

I glanced at my diploma. The contents of the safe behind it had always been the heart of e-Antiquity's future, but the blood was quickly draining from the system. Without substantial cash to fund protracted archeological pursuits, that safe just held a trivial amount of money and a folder full of old paper.

Dizziness hit me like a sucker punch.

And with the SEC on our ass, they were clearly onto Jack's mismanagement.

Would this kill me too?

A prickling quiver shot through me. I couldn't let that happen. I'd worked too hard and sacrificed too much, having my name mentioned with some of the greatest treasure hunters and archeologists in history, to watch bean counters squander it now.

I dialed a number I knew even better than Heather's.

"Buck! I've been waiting to hear from you," my father said. "Congrats on Cozumel, Son. Very impressive—"

"Thanks, Dad. It was a rush, for sure." I bit the nail on my thumb. "You around tomorrow?"

"No—I guess you haven't had the chance to check your emails. Your mother and I leave for Paris in the morning. Super busy here, with the Group of Seven—"

"I need to see you, Dad. Can you come to my office? I can wait—"

"I'd love to, Son, but the secretary of state—"

"He has lots of under secretaries, Dad. He can spare you, can't he?"

"I'm in charge of these Paris meetings…."

Silence followed. I closed my eyes tight.

"However, I'll be heading back out to the farm in an hour. I haven't packed yet, so I can stop in Tyson's for a minute if it's urgent."

"It is, Dad. Thanks, I'll see you when you get here."

Maybe I should've just driven out to the family farm in Middleburg, but I didn't want to see Mom or Ben. Hell, I didn't want to see Dad, either. His faith in me, the joy we'd shared at each major find… but I had no choice. He surely knew some of it already, and in any case it was time to take proactive measures to protect my future.

And that of my parents.

They'd been our original venture capitalists, having literally mortgaged the farm to invest all they had in e-Antiquity. Since they'd provided our earliest seed capital, their original investment was well below where our stock was trading now. Never having sold any, they had a significant chunk of equity in e-Antiquity today.

I closed my eyes and pictured their seventy-seven-acre farm outside Middleburg. Horse barns, riding rings, paddocks, equipment sheds, and a small guesthouse, it was their pride and joy.

If I lost everything, I was young enough to rebuild. They weren't.

And I could never live with myself if that happened.

29

For the next two hours I paced the office. My reflection now in the glass over the framed *Wall Street Journal* with the photograph contrasted with that former image of me atop the pile of Mayan treasure. There I was then, in khaki safari clothing, big smile, hair tousled, and surrounded by dense jungle. In my reflection now, my hair was slicked back, my pinstriped Hugo Boss suit gleamed, and corporate excess surrounded me.

The safe held my big sheaf of original documents and my stash of cash. I reached inside.

Most of the few employees who'd been here had left, many carrying bags or boxes. I turned the corner and came face to face with Tommy, the young go-getter on our logistics team who'd been so helpful on the Guatemala project. He too was holding a box.

"What are you doing, Tommy?"

He hefted the box higher and hurried past me.

"Buck?" My father's voice called out.

I found him in the reception area where he was assessing the piles of paper and strewn trash.

"What the hell's going on?"

"Let's go in the board room," I said.

I closed the door and laid the folder of documents from my safe on the table.

"Thanks for coming—"

"Is the talk about e-Antiquity true?" His face was taut.

I threw my hands up. "I don't know what the hell Jack's done, but Zilke said he took all our cash. Now the auditors are calling, the stock's dropping, the market's teetering on collapse—everything's turned to shit." I shook my head. "Bottom line, Dad, we're in big trouble."

He sat heavily in a chair. The sound of his breathing was raspy, and he began to shake his head slowly.

Tears streaked down my cheeks as I watched fear grip him.

"Your mother and I have everything invested in—"

"Sell it now," I said. "Before the news hits the press. You have a couple of weeks, max. And take this for safekeeping." I pushed the sheaf of papers across the table. Each inch it moved away from me felt like another rung down the ladder to hell. "It's the best maps and information we have on other missing treasures—it's worth a fortune."

His face twisted, deepening the wrinkles on his brow and around his eyes and mouth.

"What am I supposed to do—"

"Take it, put it somewhere safe, sell the damned stock, and go away. Take Mom and go to Paris while I stall."

We sat staring at each other in silence for several minutes. I stood first—he had his trip to prepare for, and I'd thrown him a shit ball of diversion. He followed after me into the reception area. As soon as the elevator doors opened, we both stepped in.

"I'll take action, Son, but through channels. We can't have this come back on us." His eyes were now as clear as glacial runoff. "And going forward, communicate only through ciphers—"

"I'm not Jason Bourne—"

"We could all end up in jail, if you're not careful."

"I don't know why Jack did all this, Dad, but I'm so sorry."

The floor numbers on the elevator declined rapidly.

"There's a lot you don't know about me, Son, but suffice it to say, I haven't always been a squeaky clean undersecretary of state."

I turned to face him.

He smiled grimly. "You're not the only Reilly who had a big run in his youth. Mine, however, was all under the radar."

The doors opened and a security guard stood in our path. My heart sprang into my throat when I felt a slap on my back—Dad pushing me out into the lobby. The guard entered the elevator and the doors closed behind him. Nobody else was in sight.

"Be cool, Son. *Way* below the radar." He glanced both ways. "This is about survival. If things go bad, they can go *really* bad." He sighed. "I'll be in touch."

He pulled me in for a bear hug, and I couldn't meet his eyes. I watched him walk calmly and with purpose, his black wingtips slapping against the lobby's polished marble floor.

30

THE NEXT MORNING MY FATHER CALLED.
"It's finished," he said. "All gone."
Breath stuck in my lungs.
"And we diverted our travel to pass through Geneva on the way to Paris."

His last statement hung on the line. He didn't need to elaborate. There was only one reason for him to go to Switzerland ahead of his Group of Seven meetings—to get us a numbered bank account. I couldn't say a word.

"I'll let you know after we drop the kids at the pool," he said.

It wasn't a cipher, but I knew he was referring to the sheaf of maps.

"Travel safe, Dad. Tell Mom I love her."

I couldn't bring myself to go back to the office, not yet. Instead, I binge-watched the Financial News Network, terrified I'd see a story about e-Antiquity. I needn't have worried. The news was a frenzied accounting of a system gone wild. Over-leverage, investment banks doing crazy deals, junk bonds, and worse had led to a faltering economy. Of course e-Antiquity was ill prepared to weather the brewing storm. The anchor never mentioned us, but Yahoo indicated that e-Antiquity's volume (NASDAQ symbol: EANT) was up over the average, and the price had dropped a few points. Now in the mid-teens, every basis point counted. But the stock market in general was acting like it was on Quaaludes one minute and cocaine the next. Increasing global turmoil was the perfect cover for my father to dump stock as EANT dropped in value.

I assumed that plenty of other corporate executives were making moves to cover their asses. But it felt cowardly to be sitting here in the quiet of my own home, when whatever employees we had left would be expecting answers. I wished I had some. I took a quick shower, pulled on jeans and a long-sleeved Polo shirt, and grabbed my keys.

Before leaving I checked the answering machine to see if Heather had called while I was in the shower (she hadn't), then called Chris McLean, my broker at Merrill Lynch.

"McLean here." His voice was shrill.

"Chris, it's Buck Reilly. I'd like to sell some e-Antiquity stock." I took a breath. "*All* my e-Antiquity stock."

"Hold on, Buck." The sound of his fingers on the keyboard sounded like hail on aluminum siding. "You can't."

I covered my eyes with my palm. "Because of the SEC?"

"SEC? No, you're a corporate officer, and your trading window's closed."

I gulped a breath of air. Of course. Officers of public companies can only sell stock in their companies at predetermined dates on a quarterly basis.

"The window doesn't open for another month. Do you want to put in a sell order for then?"

"Yes."

"The way things are going, it could be a lot lower, Buck. Hell, everything could be a lot lower."

"Regardless of the price. And sell all my other stocks right away. This market, ah, has me pretty freaking freaked."

Another hailstorm of clicking ensued.

"Pretty far under water, Buck. You sure?"

My chest rose and fell, once, twice, three times. "Liquidate everything. Leave it in cash."

"I'll send you a summary of the transactions later today." He hesitated. "Sorry, Buck. Everyone here was convinced that this market would turn around by the end of summer."

The date on my Rolex Submariner indicated that today was the 1st. "September says otherwise," I said.

Chris hadn't told me exactly, but as of last night Heather's and my stock holdings were already thirty percent lower than a year ago, and we'd made a lot more money in that time that must have evaporated into the ether.

Heather.

I dialed her cell phone and closed my eyes.

"Hello?"

My eyes popped open, my sharp breath like a hiccup.

"Heather! I've been trying to reach you—"

"I'm sorry, Buck, I've been swamped for what seems like forever—"

"Where are you?"

There was a lot of noise in the background. A horn honked—traffic sounds.

"Geneva, Switzerland—"

"My parents are headed there now. They'd love to see you."

"I'm leaving for Germany tomorrow—what? Hang on…" Muffled voices followed, then more road noises. Was she crossing a street? "I have to go, Buck. I'm sorry, they're waiting for me."

"Heather, listen to me. A lot's happening—"

"I'll call tonight, I promise." She shouted, "I'm *coming*!" Then, to me, "I have to go." She was quiet for a few seconds. When she spoke next, her voice sounded very far away. "I really am sorry, Buck. Goodbye."

The line went dead.

SECTION

4

WHEN THE WHIP COMES DOWN

31

I KNEW HEATHER WOULDN'T CALL. AFTER A SLEEPLESS NIGHT, I drove to the office. I got off the elevator into the shambles of our former reception area. I hurried down the corridor that ran the length of the building, cut the corner too close—scraped into the wall—righted myself and stopped in front of Jack's door. My breathing was ragged. I grabbed the handle and pushed—locked. I pounded on the solid wood.

"Open up! Jack! Open the damn door!"

I slapped repeatedly with both open palms—

"Reilly!"

I spun around to find Starky staring me down with his fists curled on his hips, his eyes cold and pinched to slits.

"What the hell you doing, man?" he said.

"The hell am *I* doing?"

I had five inches on Starky, but he'd been some kind of mercenary from the Dominican Republic, and Jack had told me he'd killed people with his bare hands.

"Mr. Dodson's not here," he said.

"How come you still are?"

Starky lifted his right fist from his hip and slowly raised it to point toward the ceiling. A small camera was mounted next to a sprinkler escutcheon.

"Boss's orders," he said.

"Where the hell is he?"

Starky stood taller, chest thrust forward.

"I don't know."

"Let me in his office."

"Can't do that."

"What're you talking about?"

"Under orders—"

"I'm the president of this company—"

"I don't care if you're president of the United States."

I jammed a finger straight at him. "You're fired!"

Starky's squint narrowed. "You can't fire me—"

I brushed past him and strode into the human resources department. Kristina Binda was still here—I'd seen her yesterday, sitting with people as they cleaned out their desks. Yes, she was in her office, on the phone.

"Kristina!"

She dropped the phone.

"I've fired Starky. I want him removed from the premises immediately. Call building security, hell, call the cops if need be."

Starky had arrived and was staring at us without emotion.

"Write him a check for two weeks' severance. Now!"

Kristina was an attractive African-American woman, mild-mannered and very politically correct. She began shuffling papers around on her desk like she was sorting through playing cards. I held my breath, fearing she'd say Starky couldn't be fired, but she didn't.

In my late teens I'd been a Golden Gloves boxer with modest success, and while I didn't win every fight, I could almost always read my opponent's will. I saw in Starky's eyes that he wasn't going to fight.

He looked from Kristina to me. "What about my stock grants?"

I patted him on the shoulder. "Good news, you can keep 'em."

32

AFTER RIFLING KATIE'S DESK FOR A KEY AND FINDING NOTHING, I stared at Jack's solid wood door. I stepped forward and kicked just below the handle—hard—then again.

The wood creaked but didn't give.

I kicked again—and again—nothing. I glanced down the hall. Nothing.

Dammit.

In the kitchen I found a hefty fire extinguisher by the stove.

My entire body vibrated as I smashed the butt of the red canister against the door. Finally it swung wide and banged against the wall with a loud crash.

Straight ahead of me was Jack's desk. No piles of paper there—just memories of Jack seated at his pristine desk, of us laughing over details of my exploits in the field or of his updating me on new investors and the millions we were raking in.

Jack's wall safe was wide open, the picture of his family that normally covered it lying on its side against the wall.

Ransacked, or cleaned out?

The room was dry and hot. The leaves on his large corn plant drooped and had turned brown on the ends.

"Whoa! What the heck!"

Ron Zilke had come running. The sound of me kicking open the door must have reverberated through the office.

"Ron, when's the last time he was here?"

Zilke shrugged. "Maybe a week, week and a half."

Every drawer in Jack's desk was partially open. I pulled the bottom one out. It was empty. His laptop was gone from its cradle, and a cord hung from the monitor like a snake with a severed head. Other file drawers were partially full, but there were several file folders left empty.

Nothing was in the safe. Just yesterday I'd cleaned mine out—had Jack done the same?

"I told you, he ain't coming back," Ron said.

RING! RING!

Jack's desk phone rang—we both jumped.

RING! RING!

Who the hell—I stepped forward and grabbed it, my breath short.

"Jack Dodson's line."

"Mr. Reilly?"

A woman's voice—it sounded familiar—

"It's Kristina, from HR." She cleared her throat. "Um, there are some people out here—in reception. A lot of people, actually. Um, you need to come out, please."

My eyes trailed over to Zilke, whose head tilted in close so he could hear the conversation. His breath reeked of booze.

"We'll be right there," I said.

33

MEN IN DARK WINDBREAKERS FILLED THE RECEPTION AREA, some with FBI and others with SEC stenciled on the back.

"Dear God," Ron said.

An FBI man of about forty with salt-and-pepper hair stepped toward me. He did not extend his hand.

"Are you Charles Reilly the Third?"

"I am."

He thrust an envelope at me. "We have a warrant to search the premises and seize records, computers, cell phones, and servers."

"Ah, okay. Why?"

Another man of about the same age and build wearing wire-framed glasses moved next to the FBI agent.

"Dennis Johnson. I'm from the SEC's Investigative Division." He handed me another envelope. "We're here to shut e-Antiquity down. Trading of your stock is suspended at this very moment."

"But why?" I said. "For what?"

A shriek sounded behind me.

I nodded in that direction. "Ron Zilke, e-Antiquity's CFO."

"We have evidence of fraudulent reporting going back several years," Johnson said.

"Where's Jack Dodson?" the FBI agent said.

"That's a damn good question," I said.

Neither man betrayed surprise or emotion. Beyond them, a dozen or so other men and one woman stood ready, holding bins, bags, and boxes. They reminded me of a college football team waiting in the tunnel before a big game, chomping on their mouth guards, anxious to tear their opponent to shreds.

"It'll be best if you cooperate," the FBI agent said.

Ron spoke up. "Am I under—arrest?" His voice broke.

The SEC man grimaced. "Not yet."

"But don't go anywhere," FBI said.

I shuffled out of the way, against the wall, and the federal team poured out of the figurative tunnel, the crowd cheering in my mind as they stormed into our main corridor, with half the players running in one direction and the others running the opposite way.

BRRAALLPPH!

Zilke had thrown up all over the carpet, right by the FBI agent's feet. The man's shoes and lower pants legs were splattered with barf. The smell of Scotch mixed with French fries curled my nostrils.

"Hell's bells!" the agent said.

"Mr. Reilly?" Johnson said. "Please come with me."

He led me into the conference room and closed the door. The smartest thing to do would be to call my attorney—but I only had business attorneys. Would their firms have criminal defense teams? I swallowed.

Through the glass I could see Ron Zilke on his knees trying to wipe the puke off the FBI agent's feet, but the man was stepping back and waving him off.

"So you have no idea where Jack Dodson is?" Johnson said.

"Look, I'm freaking out here, know what I mean? I just got back from Mexico, what, a couple of days ago?"

"Cozumel, yes, we know."

"Right, and when I came in here, I found…well, you know."

"No, sir, I don't know. What did you find?"

"Chaos, that's what I found! Fucking chaos." I leaned forward. I wasn't sure whether I felt or smelled the sweat that had soaked my armpits. "Jack hadn't returned my calls in a week. He was gone. Most of our staff was gone—quit, or fired, I don't even know, and, hell… I just kicked Jack's door open a few minutes ago."

His expression never changed. He just stared at me. "Why'd you do that?"

"Looking for answers, dammit! What the hell's going on? What happened? I mean, shit, one minute we're on top of the world and then—well, here you are."

"So you don't know Jack Dodson's whereabouts?"

"Have you tried his house?"

"FBI agents are there now." He stared at me for a long moment. "Yours too."

"Mine? What the hell for?"

"Is Mrs. Reilly at home to let them in? The FBI has a warrant—"

"For my house? A warrant?"

He held my gaze.

"No, she's not there," I said. "Nobody's there. Should I go let them in?"

Was he trying not to smile? "They'll let themselves in," he said.

My breathing was shallow. I wished Johnson would quit staring at me. I used my sleeve to wiped perspiration off my forehead.

"Do I need an attorney? Am I under arrest?"

"We're not here for arrests."

Yet. The silent word was clear. Oh, God—would they know about my parents selling their stock yesterday?

The door opened. It was the lead FBI agent.

"Come with me, Mr. Reilly."

Out in the reception area I dodged an agent pushing a cartful of paper, followed by another, then another, all with carts loaded to the top with computers and electronics. They were gutting our offices in record time.

"This way," FBI said.

I stepped over Ron Zilke's barf and followed the agent into Jack's office, where at once he turned to face me. Two other agents were waiting, staring at the desk and files, then back at me, waiting like Doberman Pinschers who'd been told to sit. "Is this your office?" FBI said.

"No, it's Jack's."

"And you broke in here?" Johnson said.

"Yeah, just before you arrived."

"And why'd you do that?" FBI said.

"Because, well, he wasn't here, he hasn't returned my calls, I just found out he's lied about everything, and now everyone's gone. There are SEC stamps all over our records—I don't know what the hell's happening, that's why."

FBI glanced around the room checking his Dobermans, still frozen, awaiting orders. "Looks like he left in a hurry."

At the wall safe, FBI used a blue BIC pen to swing the door open wide. "What did he have in here?"

I held my hands up. "I don't know where Jack is, I don't know what he kept in there. Can't you find him? Is he home? Johnson said you had people there now. Ask them, okay?"

"Agent Frazier?" Another agent had poked his head inside Jack's office. "We found another safe, sir."

My office was the only other one with a safe in it.

Frazier, that was the lead agent's name. He stared at me for a long moment, then, without taking his eyes off me, addressed his men.

"Proceed."

Of course they leapt into action. Kick-off team, ready to pound it deep.

"Please come with us, Mr. Reilly."

I followed, but I could have led the way.

34

INSIDE MY OFFICE WERE TWO FBI AGENTS. THEY'D ALREADY removed my computer and were taking all the files from the drawers and placing them in boxes and then transferring the boxes to carts. My diploma leaned against the wall on the floor.

Agent Frazier walked in. "Can you confirm that this is your office, Mr. Reilly?"

"That's my name on the diploma. Those are pictures of me—that's my father in that one—Under Secretary of State Reilly."

"We know who he is," Frazier said. "So this is your safe?"

I just nodded. Sarcasm would get me nowhere, and anger often made me say things I soon regretted.

"We need you to open it up, please."

After they moved aside, it took me three tries to get the safe open, my fingers trembled so much. Frazier pulled the envelope out and placed it on my desk. One of the other agents took pictures of the envelope, then Frazier pulled it open.

"There's more than twenty thousand dollars in cash here." He said it as he might have said the envelope contained twenty thousand pieces of stationery.

"Like I said, I travel a lot. I need cash for…transactions."

"Has anything been removed from here in the past week?"

I subconsciously groaned, then used the sleeve of my right arm to again wipe my forehead. "I told you I just got back in town from Mexico, so, no."

"Why Mexico?" Frazier said. "A lot of money laundering down there."

"It was an archeological dig in conjunction with the University of Mexico." His flat stare caused me to ball my fist. "There were plenty of reporters there with us. Feel free to look it up."

"Don't worry, we will."

Within another hour the team of Feds had cleaned out every office and taken every computer or piece of equipment that had electronic memory. Ron Zilke, with fresh Scotch in hand, watched with me from the board room as the teams disappeared into the elevators with full carts, only to return a few minutes later with empty ones. Kristina Binda and the other people who had been here were relieved of their cell phones and asked to leave. Only Ron and I remained. Johnson and Frazier returned, accompanied by the one female agent who now held a thick roll of yellow tape.

"Need you men to leave now," Frazier said. "This is now considered a crime scene. We'll be sealing off the entrance. Nobody will be allowed back here until we've gone through all the confiscated materials." He glanced behind him to where another agent stood by a cart full of electronic equipment.

"One other thing." Frazier pointed to an agent next to a half-full bin. "We removed the digital recorder from your security officer's console."

I recalled Starky pointing to the camera in the ceiling in front of Jack's office. A chill passed over me, made worse since my shirt was so damp with perspiration. I glanced up and noticed a camera mounted in the ceiling by reception, and here too, in the board room. Was there a camera in my office?

"Mr. Reilly?" Frazier said.

"Excuse me?"

"I asked if you know where the security tape is that was last in the recorder. We found six months' worth of different tapes in a locked cabinet, leading all the way up to last week, but the machine itself was empty. Can you tell us why?"

My stomach flip-flopped.

"I have no idea."

"Where's your security director?" Frazier said.

"He, ah, no longer works here."

Frazier's stare gave no hint whether he thought I was a lying piece of crap, or telling the truth.

He said, "His tapes were neatly filed up until—"

"I fired him earlier today. He refused to open Jack's office for me. I'm the president of the damned company."

"I see. Okay, we'll have your HR director provide us with his contact information." He nodded to the man with the security gear in his cart. "All right, gentlemen, time to call it a day."

"Day?" Ron Zilke said. "More like career."

The two of us walked out of the room, Ron none too steadily. If Jack had him cooking the books, then he could easily do time for that. Jack, too, of course, but what about me? Could I go to jail for their fraud? I was an officer of the company, and ignorance isn't much of a defense.

Frazier had stopped in front of the elevator.

"Mr. Zilke, Mr. Reilly, we need you both to remain local until you hear otherwise. Understand?"

We both nodded. No point in arguing that my role within the company was to travel—we didn't exactly *have* a company any more. The yellow "POLICE LINE - DO NOT CROSS" tape they stapled across the door made that clear.

I had to find Jack. What the hell had he done?

35

THE ENSUING TWENTY-FOUR HOURS WAS LIKE A BAD ACID TRIP. My house looked as if a tornado had blown through it, thanks to the FBI's search. I'd spent the night on the couch in front of the TV where news of e-Antiquity's shut-down, with footage of the FBI wheeling carts out of our building, had been a top story on multiple networks.

Didn't CNN have something more important to cover?

Had I slept at all? Couldn't be sure, for facts and nightmares, equally unpleasant, had synthesized into the same reality. Daylight invaded from around the edges of my closed shades, and with two news trucks parked on the road in front of my house I wouldn't be leaving any time soon. Fortunately, my driveway was two-tenths of a mile long, with a NO TRESPASSING sign at the end, so they couldn't pull right up to my house and pound on the front door.

Opinions on social media had been vicious, some referring to e-Antiquity as the tip of the iceberg for an economy on the brink of collapse. But ninety-nine percent of opinions are uninformed garbage spewed by people with nothing better to do. If not for the archeological relics we'd uncovered around the world, however, e-Antiquity's only legacy might have been as a morally corrupt, fraudulent footnote erased from the New York Stock Exchange like a bastard child.

On-line versions of *Wall Street Journal, Washington Post, New York Times,* and *Discover* magazine universally skewered us as modern-day pirates, some even questioning my background and qualifications to be included with leading archeologists, discoveries be damned. As treasure hunters, we'd always battled that reputation, even in good times.

Scrounging for food, I drummed up some frozen waffles and turned the sound up on the local news. Breaking news on e-Antiquity—I dropped my fork.

Video from Jack Dodson's house showed his wife, Laurie, crying hysterically as an FBI agent escorted her into a government sedan, while their housekeeper held her kids back and newsmen shoved microphones in her face. Mercifully, no sound was carried on the video, but the reporter said: "…CEO Jack Dodson is still missing…" and added that the FBI had already been to Dodson's house, where they had removed "several articles of interest." Video rolled of what I was certain were the same white laundry carts they had in our office being wheeled out of Dodson's house to unmarked vans. Special Agent Robert Frazier—they showed him watching the procession of carts from the entry stoop—refused to comment on the investigation.

And Heather had never called back as she'd promised.

Son of a bitch.

Would they discover that I'd given valuable company property to my father?

What had happened to that security tape in the recorder?

They'd certainly see that my parents had sold their stock just before our crash, but could they prove insider trading?

I'd not yet contacted an attorney but had searched insider trading penalties on-line, and the maximum sentence was up to twenty years—

DING-DONG!

What the hell?

The news people had been given explicit instructions to stay away—

DING DONG!

Dammit!

I caught a glance of myself in the mirror—hair awry, unshaven, bathrobe cinched tight. I wasn't going to answer the door, but I peeked through the peephole...

No.

Two men in dark suits stood outside. One held credentials up to my peephole. The logo of the Federal Bureau of Investigation stared me in the eye.

"Open the door, Mr. Reilly," the man with the credentials said. "We know you're in there."

Shit!

I peeked again—they stared straight at the peephole.

I smoothed my hands down the front of my robe, then reached for the deadbolts and door handle. Screw it.

"Good morning, gentlemen." I glanced past them and saw a lot of activity at the end of my driveway—probably telephoto lenses peering through the woods. "Forget something yesterday?"

"You're under arrest, Mr. Reilly. We're taking you downtown."

My knees buckled—my bathrobe flew open, exposing my tighty-whities underneath—one of the agents grabbed my arm. They led me to a chair by the front door where I sat heavily.

One read me my Miranda rights as I tried to catch my breath. Suddenly I flashed back to being in the cell in Tortola and felt as if my body turned to jelly—I couldn't sit up straight. No way I wanted to go back to jail.

The other agent appeared with a glass of water. After guzzling it down, I sat up straight and pulled the robe together.

"Get on some clothes, Reilly."

Once dressed, I was led outside—uncuffed—one of the Feds right in front of me and one right behind. It wasn't like I could run. There was no place to hide—people knew me all over the world.

After all, I was King-freaking Buck.

36

THE AGENTS TOOK ME TO THE FBI'S WASHINGTON HEADQUARTERS where, after being ushered from a secure parking garage through a labyrinth of corridors and up a couple of floors, I found myself in an interrogation room equipped with mirrored windows, furniture bolted to the floor, and painfully bright lighting.

My world had become a free fall to black. I hadn't even considered who I'd use for an attorney if it got worse, and now that it had, none of the ones who came to mind were criminal defense lawyers.

The door swung open to admit Special Agent Frazier. The door closed quickly after him.

CLICK.

I distinctly heard the sound of the lock being engaged from the outside. Frazier had a folder with him, which he placed on the far end of the table.

"I have questions, Reilly—"

"What about an attorney?"

"That's your right, of course." He stared at me, seated in the metal chair, as if I were a terrorist, bank robber, kidnapper, or syndicate boss.

An urge to vomit bent me forward, but nothing came up.

"But before you call your attorney, I want you to know I'm willing to make you a deal."

Deal? Hell, I'd sell my soul not to go to jail—a bloom of perspiration hit—but I'd already sold my soul to succeed and was here as a result.

"Where's Jack?" I said.

"You really don't know?"

"Know what? That he screwed me and the company? Yeah, I've got a pretty clear picture about that now."

He continued to stare at me, and his eyes bored into mine.

"It's official," he said. "Dodson's missing. We've been questioning his wife and she appears to know nothing, but she's every bit as liable as he is, and furious about it. Their house was clean—too clean. Some of his clothes were gone, and so were some suitcases."

"Rat bastard—"

"One of e-Antiquity's largest cash accounts has been cleared out. What do you know about that?"

I clenched my jaw. That confirmed what Ron Zilke had told me.

"I don't even have access to the accounts—" An alarm sounded inside my head and my mouth snapped shut. "I want to call an attorney."

Frazier nodded. "I'll get you a phone."

He turned away, hesitated, and glanced back.

"As soon as you lawyer up, Reilly, an unstoppable process will begin. We're still gathering evidence, but it will lead to jail, hearings, and we'll oppose bail because of your resources and international connections. Six months from now the trial process will begin, and you'll be convicted, because Dodson has made this an open-and-shut case. You could do twenty years behind bars."

He squinted at me. "If this were a movie, guy like you might get the sentence reduced, or get out early for good behavior, but in reality, man of your profile will be a target. You'll have to fight like a pit bull in a state penitentiary to stay alive."

He shook his head. I bent over and heaved—acid reflux filled my throat—I swallowed it back.

"I'm innocent, Frazier. Stupid, sure, but I didn't know shit!"

He stepped back toward me. A long moment passed as he stared at me without blinking.

"Before you call that lawyer, I'm going to tell you a few things, then we can both decide how to proceed."

I asked for water, and a minute later a glass of it appeared in the hand of another agent entering the room. Frazier had done nothing to make that happen, and as if I didn't already know we were being monitored, they wanted to make it obvious.

"Looks as if Dodson's been moving assets around for months, into and out of his personal accounts, and then offshore." He tilted his head, appraising me. "Either you're not as smart as you should be, or a lot smarter than your partner. I haven't decided which, but charges are being filed against Dodson for theft and fraudulent conveyance of assets, for a start."

Frazier had the best poker face I'd ever seen. He was probing, and I couldn't hide my shaking hands. The feeling of struggling to tread water overcame me. I had to steer this into the shallows.

"But?"

His eyes narrowed, and the corners of his lips angled up slightly.

"You're an officer of e-Antiquity, the president, in fact, so there's no reason to believe you won't be charged too. But you can help yourself get a lighter sentence by cooperating with me. Tell me where Dodson might be—"

"Lighter sentence for *what*? I haven't transferred funds—check them out, my bank account—"

"Was cleaned out, Reilly."

I sprang to my feet.

"What're you talking about? How—Jack did that? It's impossible!"

Frazier bent down, put his hand on the folder he'd placed on the table, and slid it toward me.

"In case you didn't read it, our warrants against you include the right to review all of your personal accounts too."

I spotted the Merrill Lynch logo atop a dozen pages in the folder. My name and Heather's were there, too. It was a summary of our accounts. My eyes fluttered as I tried to focus—something wasn't right. My checking account balance was a few hundred dollars, when normally we kept it at a hundred grand. I shuffled through the pages—savings, money market, investments, all of it close to zero.

I let the papers drop to the floor. Millions had disappeared, a few hundred remained.

"What the hell?"

Frazier moved closer. "Exactly."

"You need to trace those funds, Frazier! How could Dodson—wait—did the FBI seize my money? Where's the court order for *that*?"

He shook his head slowly. "We didn't take your money, but you better believe we're tracking it down. If you transferred it offshore, we'll get you for fraudulent conveyance of assets, as a start."

"I can't—I don't know who could have done it."

"Save the drama for the courtroom." He started toward the door. "Just like Dodson, albeit far more obviously, your money has vanished. Given the crimes perpetrated by e-Antiquity, that shows forethought."

No words formed in my head.

He stopped with his hand on the doorknob to look back at me. "We're not ready to file charges against you, yet, but between the FBI and SEC, we have a hundred people working on the e-Antiquity case. It won't take long. Think about my offer, Reilly. If you don't know where Dodson is, figure out where he is, tell me, and we'll cut a deal."

"So—" My throat constricted. I guzzled water. "I can leave?"

"For now. But remember, Reilly, you can't—no, you *won't* beat us."

I followed Frazier toward the door where other agents were waiting to lead me down and out to the street. The bright light of reality made me wince. After walking a block I hailed a cab, and the long ride out to suburbia may have been the loneliest thirty-seven minutes of my life.

37

Anger replaced the initial dizziness after Frazier had blown my mind. The media presence at the end of my driveway had doubled since the FBI took me away, and my return by taxi was met with shouts and a scramble of photographers. Once inside the house, I parked myself in the study, logged into my Merrill Lynch accounts, and confirmed what Frazier had shown me.

My anger now drove me to action. I commenced a relentless campaign of phone calls. Several messages to Heather's agency— "Please have Heather Drake contact her husband immediately."

Several messages to Heather's manager— "This is an urgent message for Heather Drake. Call home ASAP."

The voice mailbox on her cell phone was full, as usual, but I texted her: "SOS, emergency, call me ASAP. Buck."

I left messages with two of her model friends and actually reached another one, who said, "Haven't seen her in ages, but I heard she was on location in Paris."

Paris, Paris, Paris. What was her favorite hotel there? I rubbed my eyes and tried to push away the mental fog. Left Bank, no, Right Bank!

The Crillon? I checked their website. No.

The Georges V? No.

The Ritz at Place Vendôme? No.

Dammit.

I scanned a map of the Right Bank—there. The Bristol.

I dialed the number. "I'm sorry, monsieur, but Mademoiselle Drake has asked not to be disturbed."

"It's Madame Drake—Madame Reilly, actually. I'm her husband. Please ring her room and tell her I'm on the phone."

After what felt like an eternity, he returned to report she was not in her room but he promised to relay my message.

My next call was to Chris McLean at Merrill Lynch. Karen, his assistant, told me he was on the golf course, but when I insisted, she connected us via a conference call.

"Whoa, Buck, what shitty news," he said. "Are you okay?"

"No, Chris, I'm not okay. In fact, I'm freaking the hell out. All my accounts are empty—zero funds. What the hell happened?"

A metallic-sounding "tink," followed by a couple of laughs, broke the silence, then Chris came back on. "Sorry about that." His voice was a whisper.

"Did you just tee off while we were talking?" Phone tucked into my shoulder, I paced the room as if it were a cage, alternately straightening my fingers and balling them into fists.

"Listen, Buck, I was told you knew exactly what was going on—"

"Told what—by who? Where's my fucking money, Chris?"

"Slow down, man, hang on—"

"What are you saying? Dammit, *what* was I supposed to know was going on?"

"Heather, dude, your wife."

"Chris! What the hell—"

"She transferred the funds, Buck, said you'd approved the transfer. Basically closed the accounts, short of leaving some crumbs to cover the fees. She said you were relocating to Europe and had set up new accounts there—"

"I never approved shit! I want my money back, Chris— I'll sue the damn brokerage faster than you can three-putt the damn hole you're on!"

"Okay, okay, let me get off the phone and find out from Karen where the wires went. I'll get back to you the minute I know." He clicked off.

Heather transferred the funds? Closed the accounts? Europe?

What the hell was going on?

I stood there not even knowing how to *think* about it. Was still standing there when the phone rang. How the hell had Chris found out so fast? I grabbed the phone off its cradle.

"Hello? Hello?"

"Buck, it's Heather."

38

"HEATHER! WHAT THE HELL'S GOING ON?"

"We need to talk," she said.

My throat felt like I'd swallowed a burning cigar, and the taste of bile churned in my mouth. I sat down carefully in my chair and pressed the phone tight against my ear.

"Are you there, Buck?"

"I'm here."

Her exhale sent a *whoosh* over the line. "I've seen the news, so I know the FBI raided your office, Jack's house—"

"Our house, too. Laurie Dodson was taken in for questioning, and so was I."

"Yeah, well, the FBI contacted my manager, and they're looking for me, too." She cleared her throat. "This is all very upsetting."

Upsetting? No, it was catastrophic. My heart sank further with each word.

"Heather, what in God's name is going on?"

"I can't afford this kind of bad publicity." Her voice was like an arctic breeze. "My career—this will kill it, Buck. I can't—*won't*—be subjected to this scrutiny."

My eyes were pressed tightly closed. White flashes faded to yellow behind the closed lids, then darkened to blue, then black.

"I know you love your image, Heather, but what exactly are you saying?"

"I can't do this anymore." Her voice was flat, devoid of emotion. "Everything was great—the sex was the best—but then you got arrested in Tortola, and now the FBI…this is killing my career."

All my years of negotiating with friendly and sometimes antagonistic people—holders of valuables, clues, maps, and archives—had me well accustomed to recognizing when I was at an inflection point. It was just something that registered in my gut, and my gut was rarely wrong. Right now, it told me that no matter what I said, Heather's mind was made up and had been made up for weeks if not months.

The light in the room darkened, and I sank further down in the chair.

"What did you do with my money?"

"*Our* money—"

"How did you con the bank into believing I'd agreed to close the accounts?"

I heard only a steady cadence of breathing, blowing hard into the phone.

"The FBI thinks I've hidden it," I said. "Heather, I could go to jail because *you* cleaned out our accounts."

"My attorney's having documents couriered to you right now. He's had a third-party appraisal done on the house."

She rushed on before I could even take in what she'd said.

"I took the liquid assets, Buck. I've signed the house over to you, and waived my rights to your e-Antiquity stock. Based on my accountant's math, you come out way ahead—"

"Our stock's frozen! The SEC shut us down!"

"I won't be held responsible for the mismanagement of your company."

"Please don't do this, Heather—"

"I'll be staying in Europe until the FBI calms down." Her tone brightened. "Let's try and remember the good times—"

"Fuck the good times!"

"I'm sorry, Buck."

"Wait! Don't hang up—"

A series of clicks was followed by a steady high-pitched whine. The phone slipped from my hand, bounced off my chest, and tobogganed onto the floor where it broke apart. The battery dangled from a few wires, a dial tone coughed, and the lights on the keypad fluttered then went black.

I finally stood up, shuffled to the wet bar in the corner, filled a glass with ice then nearly to the top with Barbancourt Eight-Year-Old rum. It went down like Gatorade. After refilling the glass I left the study, and like a moth was drawn toward the large, brightly lit TV screen alive with images of troops in the Middle East. The sound was still muted.

Oh, Heather. You're a sexy, beautiful, good-time girl. But more than that, you're a cold, heartless, greedy bitch. With every bit as much integrity as my best friend.

I guzzled half the rum, placed the glass on the table, and lay down on the huge brown sofa. Grainy images of soldiers in desert settings had me reach for the remote to turn the TV off. The rum and my consciousness evaporated simultaneously.

39

Heather never knew about the floor safe in my closet. Not because I didn't trust her, she just hadn't been home when I'd had it installed. To my relief, somehow the FBI had missed it, because it was filled with cash and copies of the original treasure maps, letters, and research materials I'd given my father. I didn't take time to count the cash, but it filled a shoebox.

I took my cell phones (personal and business), credit cards (six of them), office security ID, passport, business cards, and everything in my wallet except my driver's license and cash and stacked it all inside the floor safe. I'd been told to stay local, so I didn't want anything that would enable the Feds to track my whereabouts.

I stared at the pile and considered writing a note to leave on my desk.

What kind of note? That kind of note.

I shuddered.

I filled my backpack with blue jeans, flannel shirts, extra underwear, a flashlight, and my shaving kit. In the basement I found my sleeping bag and my antique Smith & Wesson .22 caliber revolver, which I stowed inside the old red rucksack that was once my grandfather's. I skipped my normal pre-travel routine of checking the house to make sure the doors and windows were locked and that our—my—personal effects were stored safely.

I left without looking back.

Once I sped past the gauntlet of news trucks at the bottom of the driveway, I headed toward the Washington Beltway. To avoid drawing any more attention to myself than a black Porsche 911 Turbo usually gets, I kept to the speed limit on a course north that took me through Maryland, Delaware, and New Jersey. I paid in cash for gas and all the tolls and continued through New York, Connecticut, Massachusetts, and New Hampshire. I got more gas, then crossed the Maine state line. The trip, which could have taken me around ten hours, this time took twelve.

Music from the radio filled my head. No talk radio, news, not even traffic channels, because I didn't want to hear any mention of reality. I put in two and a half more hours driving north through Maine past Freeport, Augusta, Bangor, and then Brewer before I reached Route 9. After another hour and a half I took the Northfield Road toward Machias and turned left on Little Seavy Road. It was a washboard logging road, and I drove slowly through miles of dense forest, only turning twice onto other unmarked gravel roads until I came to the end.

Collecting all my camping gear, I found and followed a narrow trail into the woods and was immediately swarmed by mosquitoes. I'd brought no protection, so I jogged over the rough, storm-rutted gullies down toward Round Lake, which soon appeared through the trees.

The half-mile path was overgrown, but I could see the moss-green cabin not far ahead. A wave of nostalgia washed over me—The 30-30 Club. My grandfather and several of his friends had built the cabin in the 1930s as a deer-hunting camp. Later, my father, grandfather, Ben, and I had come here every summer, and it was here that I'd learned to fish and shoot. In the red rucksack I found the key to the old Master padlock on the front door and stepped into a world with no phones, electricity, or plumbing, only a wood-burning stove, gas lights, and an old refrigerator fueled by a liquid propane tank.

Here, in the wilds of Maine, I intended to lose myself.

I got the propane on and attempted to start the refrigerator, which coughed black smoke several times before the pilot light finally lit.

With a chill in the air, I built a fire, and the crackle of dry wood kept me company along with the mice I'd spotted dashing along the open wood rafters. The camp consisted of two rooms, one a kitchen with a hand pump for water from the lake, the other a room with six stacked bunks, two-by-two, and another against the wall where the cook slept during hunting season.

From the camp on its hill above the lake a panoramic view spread out below me. The lake wasn't large, maybe seven hundred acres, and given its remote location, harbored only a few other camps on its shores. The East Machias River ran through it, providing a steady flow of pickerel, perch, and bass. Our old Alumacraft boat was chained to a tree near the water, and the six-horsepower Johnson outboard was in the storage shed. With the sunset sky beginning to swirl with pinks and purples, getting on the water would have to wait until tomorrow.

Even though I was exhausted from the trip, I took all the cash from my safe and wrapped it in plastic bags from the kitchen, then rummaged in the storage shed and found an old metal toolbox to hold the bags of cash. I then carried it, with a shovel, twenty paces to the east of the outhouse and dug a hole, wrapped the toolbox in more plastic, and buried it under enough dirt, stones, and pine needles to make the place indistinguishable from its surroundings. Finally, I scattered the excess dirt in the woods.

That night, by the fire, I studied the old maps tacked to a board on the wall that showed Maine Townships 18 and 19. Topographic lines detailed the hills and streams, and other lakes and landmarks were all named. On the table next to me sat a glass of rum, neat, and my Smith & Wesson.

Would the FBI be searching for me?

The SEC?

Heather's attorney?

Or my parents—I hadn't had the heart to contact them but guessed they must have heard the news. Would they get in trouble for selling their stock? Could they voluntarily return the money they'd cashed out to avoid prosecution? The likelihood that I'd brought shame on my father that could ruin his career at the State Department was too painful to think about.

As I sat there and sipped rum, I became fascinated by the old revolver. Its black metal reflected flickers from the stove's open door, and six gray bullets peeked from the individual open cylinders, their copper jackets visible on the opposite end. It was light in my hand, its barrel short, designed more for close-up use than distance.

A .22 didn't have much punch. A bullet would have to be placed just right to kill a man.

I could imagine how someone who'd lost everything might put this gun to use.

My finger was loose on the trigger.

I'd lost everything.

I stared down the barrel.

But I'm not that guy.

The wind suddenly rattled the windows, and a gust blew out through the stove's front door, extinguishing the propane light above my head.

I shivered. Enough.

I put the gun down on the table, drained my glass of warm rum, closed the door on the stove, and shuffled through the darkness to my sleeping bag in one of the lower bunks.

Tomorrow would come soon enough.

40

Morning light came early. With no blinds to screen the sun, it was in my face at 5:45. A sharp pressure in my bladder urged me to move, but a pounding behind my eyes kept me inside the sleeping bag. I dozed off again, tossed around the bunk—my dreams were disjointed, like a carnival mirror—and woke up long enough to look at my watch on the shelf. *What?*

It was 9:15. I sat up—my head ached even worse. The room spun, and nausea hit me—I rolled to the edge of the bunk and threw up onto the gray-painted wood floor.

What the hell?

A kaleidoscope of colors danced across my mind—another thirty minutes passed—I was staring up at the bottom of the bunk above me. A crisscross of metal webbing supported the ancient mattress. My head rolled to the side, and my eyes gradually focused on the eaves of the camp where the pair of propane-fueled lights hung down above the stove. I traced the light fixtures' contours with my eyes—something was wrong. Each light was controlled by an L-shaped switch that if pointed down meant the propane feed was off, and if up, the feed was on. The mantle on the light above the wood-burning stove wasn't lit, but its switch was up.

My eyes fluttered—then bugged wide. Pain shot through my head, and I suddenly knew why.

Last night's wind that had blown through the open stove door and extinguished the light. I'd failed to turn the switch off, so the fuel feed, of course, had stayed on. I struggled to my feet. The smell of soot filled the cabin. Even more alarming was a gray haze hovering in the kitchen—a thin gray plume puffed steadily from the rear exhaust on the refrigerator!

After shutting off the gas and opening every window and door, I stood outside panting heavily. My heart raced, my breathing was shallow, and my head felt like a deflated punching bag.

I could have died.

And if I had, people would have assumed I'd done it on purpose.

The wind rustled the long pine boughs, a pair of loons called to each other across the lake, the swirl of a fish left a ring in the water near the shore.

I wanted to live, dammit.

Carbon monoxide poisoning should require blood tests to determine the extent of the damage, and if the CO_2 counts were high enough, I'd need a stint in a hyperbaric chamber to correct the oxygen level. I should have called 911 and Poison Control, but none of that was going to happen. Nobody knew I was here, and I intended to keep it that way.

I pushed through the dizziness and pain, managed—very slowly—to drag the boat into the water and fix the outboard motor on the transom. Then I sat for a good while just breathing in all that pristine Maine air, went to grab my old tackle box and rod from the shed, and shoved off into the clear peat-colored water. It took several hours, a grand slam of catching every species of fish in the lake, and spotting two bald eagles and a cow moose before I felt human again. That, plus a fry-up of freshly caught bass and white perch, washed down with some Wild Turkey I found on a kitchen shelf, did the trick.

Two more days passed, with me surviving on food I'd caught and running out of rum and whisky before square decisions finally fell into the square holes of my life.

Heather was gone. The money was gone. Jack and e-Antiquity were gone. King Buck was worse than gone, a laughingstock at best and a jailbird-to-be at worst. All thanks to the man who had been my best friend all my life.

Maybe the fresh Maine air—or the fishing, fresh meals, and blue skies—led me to make an outrageous decision.

A gut-punch of guilt made me flinch. My parents would be worried sick over my disappearance. I didn't want to jeopardize them further, or draw attention to their stock sale, by calling them. And I still wasn't ready to talk to them, even to tell them I was okay. I spent one last afternoon in the quiet of the camp, the only sound indoors the sharp crackle of cedar kindling and white birch logs.

After a quick cleanup that evening, I used my flashlight to guide me through the black woods to my car in the gravel clearing. Fourteen hours later I was on the Capitol Beltway in morning rush hour. But instead of heading west on Georgetown Pike toward home, I took I-66 into Washington and found my way to an iconic building where two stout men in security uniforms manned a metal detector at the main entrance.

"That's right," one of the men said into his phone, "Charles Reilly the Third is here to see you." His eyes stayed on me. "He's standing right here in front of me, showing me your card. You want to see him or not?"

A big smile came over his face. "No problem." Then, to me, "Please sit right over there where I can see you, Mr. Reilly. He'll be right down."

41

Frazier arrived in an elevator full of FBI agents. He marched toward me, his dark-gray suit pressed smooth, the blue-and-white striped tie bright against his starched white shirt. No windbreaker here at headquarters.

"Where the hell have you been, Reilly?" He spoke before he reached me, then stopped to prop balled fists on his hips.

"Don't get all worked up—"

"I told you to stay in contact!"

"I went fishing."

Fishing? He mouthed the word.

I nodded. "My wife dumped me and my company's broke. I needed some time."

He straightened up, narrowed his eyes, and let out a long breath.

"Let's go upstairs."

We took the elevator with our entourage of three other agents and entered another interrogation room. I'd come here of my own volition and had a plan, so I felt confident. I took a seat and looked up at Frazier, whose eyes were hooded and his lips pinched.

"Have you seen the news?" he said.

I shook my head. "Did you catch Jack?"

He leaned forward and rested his palms on the table, staring into my eyes. What was that I saw in his?

"I'm sorry, Reilly, but your parents are dead. They were killed in a hit-and-run in Geneva."

My vision suddenly shrank to a binocular view that zoomed in on Frazier's mouth and eyes, both taut.

The air froze in my lungs. "No!"

As his face twisted in response to mine, my limbs turned to jelly and I slid off the chair.

Long lines of fluorescent illumination shimmered in a hazy blur of brilliance against a gray backdrop. A white beam moved toward my face—my eyes suddenly watered—ammonia!

I shook my head—my vision clicked back on and I saw several men in the room. One younger woman, attractive, loomed over me. She drew her hand back.

"Thanks, nurse," a male voice said.

I glanced past the woman in the white dress to see Special Agent Frazier.

The long drive, the Beltway, the monuments in Washington, walking away from my parked—where was my car? The Hoover Building—I'd come to see—

My parents were dead?

A screech of air caught in my throat. My eyes focused on Frazier's.

Or was that a nightmare?

"Where are my parents?" I said.

"Switzerland. Per their Last Will and Testaments, their bodies have been cremated."

When I burst into tears, I saw him wince. After that, I fought to suppress the sobs that shook me, and Frazier helped me to my feet and led me to another interrogation room. Once I was seated, he offered me coffee or a Coke. I asked for water.

"Where were you fishing, Reilly?"

"Why does it matter?"

"You haven't used any credit cards—"

"I used what cash I had on hand."

"Where's all your money?"

"My wife left and cleaned me out." A quick mental flash back to the hole near the outhouse in Maine.

"Interpol might find that convenient," Frazier said.

"Her leaving me is *convenient*?"

"Interpol wants to question you, Reilly. They think you may have had something to do with your parents'—"

When I leapt out of my seat, fists balled, he took a step back. The other two men moved closer, ready to grab me.

"Are you fucking demented? You just tell me my parents were killed by hit and run, and now you're suggesting— check my passport, I'm sure you have access to the U.S. Customs data base."

"All I said is, they want to question you."

I paced around the room, rubbing my face with both hands. This couldn't be happening!

Mom and Dad? Dead? In Switzerland? "Does my brother know?"

"Bound to. It's been all over the news."

They'd diverted to Switzerland for me, to stash my archives. No! Please, that can't be what happened—

"Reilly?" He sounded conciliatory now. "Why'd you come here?"

I drank from the glass of water on the table.

"To take you up on your offer—I'll cooperate."

"Dodson?" Frazier said. "You know where he is?"

I shook my head and sat down. "No idea, but I'll damn sure try to find out."

The next sixty minutes or so were a barrage of questions about e-Antiquity, our finances, investors, accounts, who had access, signing rights, on and on. Aware that my limited knowledge of these topics sounded suspect, or even pathetic for the president of the company, I patiently explained again that all financial control and management had been left to Jack Dodson and his finance team.

"My job was to find treasures we could use to establish an international reputation as a world-class archeological firm, and then ultimately monetize. No product, no company."

"No money, no company," Frazier said.

Not funny, but I kept my mouth shut and propped my chin on a fist.

"How much did Dodson abscond with?" Frazier said.

"I have no idea—Ron Zilke, our CFO, said several million. We'll get the banks to—"

"Already in process. Stay away from your former banks. They've been advised not to speak with anyone from e-Antiquity."

The quiver in my gut that began soon after I'd regained consciousness was spreading to my legs and arms. A tic fluttered in my right eyelid, and I couldn't look directly at Frazier. My mind drifted through a montage of images of my mom laughing, gardening, riding her horse…and my dad, wearing a suit, shooting his shotgun at a pheasant, fishing…but I kept coming back to my dad's face in the conference room when I told him e-Antiquity was doomed.

My cheeks burned, and when I felt a tear fall on my fist I sat up straighter and wiped my face with my palms.

"I can't continue with this right now." My voice was a whisper. "So again, am I under arrest?"

Silence followed, and I saw Frazier exchange nods and tilted-head looks with the other two men in the room, neither of whom had uttered a sound.

"We know your father sold all his e-Antiquity stock the day before we shut you down."

I held his gaze. "On the bottom. Is there a law against that?"

"You can go today, Reilly, but let me be perfectly clear. Do *not* leave the area, do *not* disappear, and do *not* go fishing again." His gaze bored into mine. "Right now, you need to find Dodson."

"How am I supposed to—"

"You're King Buck, that's how. You find lost civilizations, you can find your partner."

"Lost civilizations aren't on the run with millions in their pocket."

"And stay by your phone—where's your cell?"

"At home."

"Go there, and I'll be in touch—or call me if you learn anything about Dodson's whereabouts."

I was led through the same bland corridors as last time, my feet numb on the epoxy floor. As I walked toward the rectangular pools of light that led to the street, tears flooded my eyes to stream down my face. Outside, I stood for a moment, trying to remember where I'd parked—

"Buck Reilly?" A voice called from in front of me.

I looked up into a blinding floodlight.

"King Buck, can you explain to our CNN audience why you're back in the Hoover Building?"

What the hell?

I stepped forward with an arm thrown over my eyes against the glare. It helped shield me from the camera flashes, but I'd never find my car that way.

The reporters were relentless. "Is there any connection between the fall of e-Antiquity and the death of your parents—"

The blazing lights still obscured my vision, but I spun around and took off down the street with no idea where I was going. Just away from the press, away from the FBI I'd come in to help.

No good deed goes unpunished.

42

Home may be where the heart is, but right now it was just a box of bricks containing my landline phone, useless credit cards, and photos of the woman who'd left me. Ben was my only family now, and regardless of Agent Frazier's admonition that I should go home, I needed to see my brother. Sick that he'd been dealing with this news all by himself, I pushed the Porsche at high speed out Route 66.

But first I had another stop to make.

News trucks clogged the McLean streets as I approached, and I didn't give a damn if they recognized my car. I pulled in next to the lone car in the driveway. By the time I got out, a press contingent three deep was lined up on the street.

"Buck Reilly!"

"Come talk to us!"

"Turn around!"

Camera shutters clicked behind me like swarming cicadas.

Laurie Dodson opened the door and pulled me inside.

"Where the hell is my husband?"

Her face was drawn, with heavy bags under her eyes. Her clothes were rumpled, and the house looked as if looters had gutted it. A child's crying shrilled from upstairs.

"That's what I came to ask you—"

WHACK! When she slapped me, I jerked back, my left ear ringing like a gong.

"That's for St. Barths. You're both pigs."

I rubbed my cheek. "I had no idea this was coming, Laurie, and I need to find Jack. We'll all go to jail—"

"Not me." She shook a fist at me. "I'll turn his ass in if I can save my children from humiliation and keep my house."

"Heather left me—"

She waved the comment off. "She was trouble anyway." Her eyes were black bottomless pits.

I swallowed, hard. "Look, Laurie, I'm as surprised as you are. I knew our stock was down, but I had no idea what a mess we were in, or that Jack would…um…disappear."

She squinted at me, both fists balled.

I said, "If you hear anything will you call me?"

"Oh, yes." She nodded. "You'll be my second call."

Back on the highway, afternoon traffic was thick as I continued west, ultimately getting off on Route 15 to take me to Route 50 and into the well-heeled community of Middleburg, where my parents had lived for most of my life.

Laurie's anger burned in my chest. Damn you, Jack.

Ben and I'd had an amazing childhood on our parents' farm, riding horses, fishing, and using Dad's metal detector to look for Civil War treasures. Four years older than my little brother, I could still picture the gleam in his eyes whenever I'd suggest various adventures. The recognition that we'd grown apart, thanks to Jack, ate at me. Ben's resentment about that remained close to the surface, even after all these years. Time to reconcile that, now that Mom and Dad were gone.

Killed by hit and run.

My fingers tingled on the steering wheel. The news of e-Antiquity had only broken a few days ago. No connection between their deaths and my company seemed to hold any water—unless someone knew they were stashing goods for me, but again, who and how? Jack? He'd run off with millions, why would he care about old documents he'd never be able to make use of?

No connection made sense, and however much my heart ached that they'd gone to Switzerland on my behalf, their deaths had to be an accident.

At Middleburg I drove through the village, on the right the Red Fox Inn where Heather and I had stayed when we came out to visit and wanted privacy—I had to look away. A few miles farther I turned left on Zulla Road, then drove another couple of miles until I reached the driveway marked only by a large black mailbox. A long line of mature oak trees provided a green canopy over the gravel lane that, after three-tenths of a mile, led to the old red brick Georgian house. Until this moment, every time I'd arrived here had sparked a sense of pride at what my parents had accomplished to afford such an amazing property. The guesthouse was near the five-acre pond, where Heather and I had skinny-dipped by moonlight the first time she'd come out to meet my parents.

Now that feeling of pride was gone, replaced by a numb emptiness. My movements shifting gears and steering felt mechanical as I parked next to Ben's white BMW X-5. He'd lived here since graduating from UVA three years ago, working a few odd jobs before starting law school at George Mason University the previous fall.

The front door swung open—Ben stood there head

down, his face shadowed, his body rigid. My heart sank as I walked toward him, tears again wet on my cheeks.

But when I reached out to hug my brother, he held his palms up and stepped back. He trembled, but I saw no tears. Instead, I saw that his eyes blazed in an unblinking stare.

"Mom and Dad have been dead for two days. Where the hell have you been?"

"I didn't know, Ben. I was at the camp—"

"Maine? Why the hell—"

"Heather left me, and the company—"

"Is bankrupt. Yeah, I watch the news."

His posture remained rigid. It was like he was blocking the door. A wave of sweat passed over me, like a bucket of spit dumped on my head.

"And you were right about Jack, all these years." I waited for his answer, and when none came, I went on. "My life's over, Ben. I'm screwed."

"Ha!" A dry, single-note laugh rocked his head back. "*Mom and Dad's lives* are over, Buck. You've just had a professional setback."

"Why are you acting like this is my fault?"

"Mom told me the morning they left that you'd given them something, and that they had to take a side trip to Switzerland before the meetings in Paris. That's why they were in Geneva, right?"

"Stop!"

"Did your errand get them killed?"

We still stood on the covered veranda between the white Doric columns that framed the mahogany door. I could see past him into the house, hear the audio from a TV news channel. The house looked dark inside.

"Why are you doing this?" I said. "We need each other—I need you."

"Why did the FBI arrest you?"

"They didn't." I pushed past him into the house.

"And Interpol wants to talk to you—hey! I live here now." His voice followed after me. "I'm not sure you're welcome—"

I turned and stepped into him. At six-three I was four inches taller than Ben, and I'd always been stronger and more athletic.

"I don't know what the hell's going on, but you need to back off, little brother." When I leaned closer his eyes met mine, unwavering. "I'm just as upset as you are. And the last thing I want is to argue with you."

He glanced down the darkened hallway toward the kitchen, where the sound of a familiar CNN news anchor's voice spoke with urgency. As always.

"Whether you care or not, Ben, I'm in serious shit. And all of this is…is…" I stepped back. "I came here because I wanted to be close to you, Mom and Dad, the only way I know how at this point." I bit my lip. "And to talk to you about getting them home and arranging a proper burial."

His face fell then, and a long exhale slumped Ben over.

I pulled him close for a bear hug, and whether it was because I'd pinned his arms to his sides or the crap about Interpol, he didn't reciprocate.

He broke free, pivoted, and disappeared into the interior darkness.

43

I WALKED THROUGH THE DARKENED HALLWAY WHERE PHOTOS stared at me from the murk. The audio from CNN got louder as I approached the lit kitchen.

"…In front of the FBI's Hoover Building today…"

Good grief, it was about me.

I hurried past and turned left into my father's study, which was also dark because the shades were drawn. With the light on the room came to life, and photos of family and his decorated career jumped off the wood-paneled walls. Golf clubs stood in the corner next to his locked gun cabinet, and the massive sixteen-point whitetail deer head that was once a Boone and Crockett Club record dominated a side wall.

I reclined in his brown leather chair and watched dust float in a narrow shaft of light seeping through the blinds. Silence crowded in on me. Atop the desk lay an old-fashioned calendar desk blotter, with notes filling each day until the 23rd, the day they'd left for Europe. My father's writing was precise and legible, something I'd always envied since a high-school teacher had compared mine to chicken scratch. But it wasn't his penmanship that caused my heart to skip, it was the note on the 22nd: "Swiss Bank / Buck."

"What the hell are you doing in here?"

Ben's voice made me jump—my knees hit the bottom of the desk drawer. "I've always loved this room. Dad's inner sanctum—"

"So why're you going through his stuff?"

"I'm just sitting here."

He stared at me, that shaft of light slicing across his face and body.

"I don't think you should be in here."

"What are you talking about?"

"Were you really at the camp?"

My jaw burned as I clenched it before responding.

"Yes, Ben. I was at the camp—caught a grand slam as a matter of fact—"

"I saw the FBI arresting you at your house on the news, and then you leaving FBI headquarters on television today."

"They took me there days ago. I wasn't arrested—they let me leave, I went to the camp, and when I came back I went back to the FBI to offer my help against Jack. This morning was when I found out about Mom and Dad. I hadn't seen the news for days."

Ben's brow furrowed. "You went back to the FBI on your own?"

As he came closer, I leaned forward with my arms over Dad's last notes.

"Their ashes are being shipped home, you know." Ben's face was haggard, his eyes narrow, his lip quivering. "I wanted to go there, but Dad had his Last Will and Testament with him, for some weird reason—any ideas about that?"

"Sure. He always traveled with both his and Mom's when overseas."

"But the State Department rep told me their bodies were so disfigured—the car that hit them had been going very fast—and the police had no interest in an autopsy, so they cremated the bodies, per their wills." He leaned against the desk now, in front of me.

Guilt ran as wild in my body as thunder-crazed horses.

"Did the FBI tell you that, too?"

I shook my head.

"That Interpol is bringing them home tomorrow? In sealed wooden urns?" His spittle shot out to land on my arms atop the desk. "Do you even care? Your *investors* are dead—"

I shoved hard against the desk, and the chair flew back. I was out and moving toward Ben, who stepped backward. As I reached for him, he shuffled his feet quickly and took another big step back as far as the hallway. I shoved the wooden door with both hands—

SLAM!

A slide of the bar into the frame and turn of the deadbolt ensured that I'd seen the last of Ben for now.

My hands trembled as I pressed them against the door.

Dammit. Why was he acting like this?

Back at the desk, I stared for a long time at Dad's written calendar entry, then peeled off the page for the month and folded it up. Of course anyone examining it could tell a page was gone. I ran my fingers over the next month's page to find that the writing from the now missing page had pressed deeply into that one, too. I didn't need to rub a pencil over it on a slant to know that the words would be clear. Crap.

Faces stared down at me from the walls—the secretary of state, the president, the Russian foreign minister—no one was smiling except Mom. There we all were at the New York

Stock Exchange, ringing the closing bell on the day e-Antiquity had gone public—stop looking at the walls!

I pulled the drawers open and found supplies, business cards, calculator, files—the deep bottom drawer was locked. It was always locked. But I knew where the key was.

On top of the deer head.

The key fit into the lock, and the cylinder turned smoothly. Inside the drawer were other boxes made from mahogany and oak—is that what their urns would be like?

Some contained mementoes from Dad's youth, others small, old, black-book-style notebooks and leather-bound journals. I put them on top of the desk. Also in the drawer were about a dozen files, holding cryptic notes, numbers—I spotted my name. I piled them on the desk too.

"Buck!" Ben called from the hallway, then pounded on the door. "What are you doing in there?"

Shit. I glanced around the room.

"Buck!"

Bam, bam, bam! He kept beating on the door.

I spun around, raised the shade a couple of feet, reached behind it to unlock the window and open it. I slid the three wooden boxes and desk blotter through, held my breath, and dropped them all at once, hearing only a subdued clatter. I lowered the window and shade, relocked the drawer, put the key back atop the deer head, unlocked the door, and opened it.

Ben stood there, hands on his hips.

"Want to tell me what you think I've done?"

"Something with your company's earnings?"

"Ben. You need to know that Jack—"

"Mom and Dad were in Switzerland on your behalf. Want to tell me why?"

My hesitation made him lean forward. "Something

inappropriate, I'm sure, and now they're dead, and even though you'll go broke, you'll inherit half—"

"Stop it! That's all bullshit—conspiracy bullshit theories."

"I called Dad's attorney to tell him you were here."

My brother had stepped backwards again, half-lit in the dark corridor.

"And?"

"He thought it was a bad idea right now."

"Fine! Fuck it. I'll leave." I started out of the room, then stopped a foot from him. My gut tightened. "I'm going to walk around the property before I go. You want to drop this crazy talk and walk with me?"

He'd stepped further into the darkness where I couldn't see his face.

"Go ahead."

The air outside was brisk as I circled around the property. Ben's anger and suspicion left me numb. What else could go wrong? I walked around the pond, then trudged through the paddock to the barn. The horses were still in their stalls—Mom wouldn't be happy. I continued out past the equipment shed and back around to the other side of the back yard. I needed to retrieve the items I'd thrown out the window of Dad's study.

Ben's statements about Interpol and the FBI had reawakened the tic in my right eyelid. Behind the garage, I hesitated. No lights were on, and the stairs to the back porch were directly in front of me. Ben couldn't stop me, but if pressed, he could testify that I took items from the house that I wouldn't want to disclose—at least the desk blotter—the boxes were just mementoes. Dad had never let us look at them before, and curiosity had overcome me. Hopefully it wouldn't kill the cat.

44

MY OWN HOUSE WAS DARK AND SMELLED OF ABANDONMENT. The refrigerator revealed moldy fruits and bread, something in a Tupperware container with two inches of hair growing on it. All of it went out in a bag to the garbage cans. A quick glance around showed that nothing had changed. I did find a binder of unfamiliar documents on the table by the front door. Heather must have given her attorney her key, or told him where the extra one was hidden outside.

That could wait.

A fat pile of mail, mostly junk, was on the floor where I'd dumped it. A Coldwell Banker brochure and card lay on top, with a hand-written note from the agent stating that she was the top residential real-estate handler in Great Falls, if I thought I might want to sell the house. The vultures had begun to swoop in.

The red light blinking on my message machine caused a brief flutter in my chest. The first message was from Special Agent Frazier asking me to call him. The second was also from Special Agent Frazier, inquiring my whereabouts. The next voice had me leaning as close to the machine as I could get.

"Buck, I just saw the news. It's Scarlet. I'm so sorry about your parents… and, ah, everything else." A deep breath. "Let me know if I can help."

I replayed her message twice, then took the next message.

"Mr. Reilly, Wolfgang Kohm calling from Geneva. This is most regrettable, but I need to speak with you about Mr. and Mrs. Reilly's remains. They have been delivered to us to prepare—" I fast-forwarded through his message. The undertaker. Nausea sat me down. I stared at the squawk box as another message played, this one from Ben asking me to call him. Two hang-ups followed, and that was it.

Rum was my only companion. Going back to that binder of documents, I found it included the divorce decree, along with Heather's accounting of our possessions and how she'd already divided them by taking our cash and leaving me with worthless e-Antiquity stock, the house, and our furnishings. It was bullshit, and I'd contest it, but at the moment I needed liquidity.

I called the hotshot realtor who'd left the brochure, and she was even more of a braggart on the phone, but I hired her anyway. She promised to come by tomorrow to put a sign up and add it to the Multiple Listing Service. Based on the comparable sales she mentioned, I might have a hundred thousand of equity coming, but her assessment of the market was bleak—no surprise, given the steady stream of bad news on the networks about the excesses of the mortgage industry. We'd paid a million-six for the property, which had been a steal, but we'd also taken a 100% mortgage, planning to pay it off with e-Antiquity stock once it rebounded off the slow decline. That had never happened, and I now had a fat mortgage with no money to cover the monthly nut.

Another glass of rum emboldened me. I used my cell phone because its auto-dial was still programmed to include Scarlet's number.

"Hello? Buck, is that you?"

"Thanks for your message, Red. It meant a lot."

Quiet followed, save for a monotonous background hum, modulating in pitch. I couldn't quite make it out.

"Is it true about Heather?" she said.

Always to the point. "Yeah, it's true. She's gone. Same with e-Antiquity. Jack fleeced me, had been cooking the books, exaggerating reports to investors. The SEC and FBI cleaned us out."

"I saw. I was shocked, after all we'd—you'd—"

"We is right. You had as much to do with our success as I did, but you never got the credit you deserved." The humming grew louder. What the hell?

"And your parents—so terrible. I mean, how could everything go so wrong all at the same time?"

I managed a bitter laugh. That was an understatement.

"How'd you like to come over, Red? I could really use some friendly—" hiccup— "company tonight."

"Are you drunk? Never mind, who could blame you." She waited a few seconds, then said, "No, Buck, I can't come over."

"I screwed up, Scarlet, big time. I should have never let you go, I—"

"Don't go there, Buck, please." When she stopped talking, the background noise intensified, followed by rustling, then a shriek. "There was a time I longed to hear that from you, believe me, but my life's different now, I've moved on."

The sound of the wailing finally registered. "Is that a baby?"

More rustling—a loud wail—I pulled the phone away from my ear.

"Yes, it is. My son. I'm with someone else now—you know him, in fact. Craig Dettra, from the Smithsonian. He said he saw you a few months ago in Cozumel. Congrats on that, by the way."

My mouth hung open.

"Buck? Listen, now's not a good time, okay? I'm so sorry about everything that happened, but we probably shouldn't talk again."

A baby?

"Buck, are you there?"

"Craig Dettra? Seriously?"

Another wail tore at my ear through the receiver. Scarlet said something else I missed, followed by a hasty goodbye.

The phone felt like a twenty-pound weight straining my biceps until I stopped trying to hold it to my head and laid it down. I walked to the bar and emptied the balance of a bottle of Havana Club Siete Años rum over fresh ice. My supply was diminishing rapidly.

Scarlet was a mother *and* with one of my archrivals. Extra icing on the shitcake.

Everywhere I turned was a mine field of pain and anguish. I paced the first floor of the house, removing pictures from the walls to lay them face down on the floor. All my former trophies of past campaigns, whether personal or business, had become painful reminders of foolish priorities, greed, lust, coveting, and ultimately failure. It was time to dismantle the shrine to greed and excess.

But then my hand stopped in mid-air. The picture in the corner of my office was a faded 5"x7" of another life altogether. Maybe twenty years ago, given Ben's and my ages.

Mom was blonde—naturally—and Dad was fit. Muscular, actually.

I remembered the day like it was yesterday. We'd been on vacation in Key West, where Dad had rented the same old house every summer. Those vacations had planted the seeds of my interest in archeology and adventure. But this picture was from a self-timed shot on the beach a few miles west, on Woman Key. Dad had rented a boat so we could snorkel along the beach, coming face to face with a small lemon shark, then two nurse sharks. The memory revived the tingles I'd felt that day, the thrill and excitement of swimming with sharks. Mom was furious, but Dad had set his camera up on some old driftwood to capture us on Shark Beach, as we'd christened it. I stared at that photo for several minutes, leaving it on the wall.

Mom and Dad.

I went to the kitchen where I'd left Dad's boxes and calendar. What if the FBI crashed in swith a new warrant? I burned the entire desk blotter, one sheet at a time, over an open flame on the gas stove, dusted up the charred embers, and fed them into the disposal.

That left the wooden boxes.

I didn't have the heart to dig through them. Instead, I went to the garage and pulled out the moving cartons saved from when Heather and I had come here, along with big plastic bins, and stuffed my most sentimental and valuable items in them along with Dad's small wooden boxes. In the end I only filled two containers.

Amazing how compact happiness can be when you've lost everything.

Once they were safe in the backseat of the Porsche, I killed the now warm glass of Cuban rum and dozed off on the couch.

Unfortunately, tomorrow held no promise of being better than today.

45

IN THE BLACK OF NIGHT, THE PHONE RANG ON MY NIGHTSTAND. Instantly awake, I lunged for it.

"Hello?"

A lengthy silence followed, but background noise on the line kept me waiting. Someone was there.

"It's Jack."

I swung my feet to the floor, sat on the edge of the bed, and turned on the light.

"What the hell? Where are you?"

"Don't worry about that, Buck. It doesn't matter—"

"What *does* matter, Jack? You've destroyed my life—all our dreams—everything I've accomplished—"

"Please—ha!" His bitter laugh made me wince. "It was always all about you, Buck. All the international acclaim, museum exhibitions in your name, the Explorers' Club medal—King Buck? *Really?*"

"So that's it, Jack? You're what, jealous? You're the CEO—or were—of a public company. That's what you always wanted—why you went to Harvard—and you figured out how to convert the treasures I'd found into millions." I was furious, and he had to know it. "It was exactly what we'd dreamed about, and you—you killed it."

"Oh, no. I ceased to matter, as far as e-Antiquity was concerned. I'd become your chief accountant. And our failure was inevitable, thanks to the market, our expenses—do you know just how much your expeditions cost?"

"Don't give me that bullshit. Zilke told me you'd been cooking the books forever! Now the FBI's up my ass and has a warrant out for you."

"And they probably have your phone bugged, so go get your cell. I'll call you back."

Click.

Son of a bitch!

I threw the receiver down and hurried into my closet. I had yet to remove my cell phone from the hidden floor safe, so I did that now and powered it up.

It showed numerous missed calls.

Buzzz.

"Are you crazy, Jack? You think you can beat the FBI and SEC?"

"Go in your bathroom and turn the shower on."

I suddenly felt paranoid. Was my entire house bugged?

"How could you do this to me, Jack?"

The sound of a deep breath and slow exhale caused feedback on the line.

"Because I'll never be a king. And I refuse to be a pauper ever again."

"You'll wind up in jail."

"I'm sorry, Buck—hard as it may be to believe, I mean it. But when it was obvious things were going down—"

"You're *sorry?*"

"Just shut up and listen. The Feds are leaning hard on Laurie—making all kinds of threats—and she's decided to cooperate with them. That's why I'm calling."

I started to say I'd seen her but clamped my mouth shut. Had Laurie left Jack, just as Heather had me? She was going to testify against him, but wait—

"I thought that was illegal—a spouse can't be forced to testify."

"I told her to. Any money I send her will be confiscated, so she needs to exonerate herself."

"And what about me?"

"That's why I called." Silence followed.

"I'm listening."

"There's no way I can avoid arrest, but a negotiated deal gives me better leverage."

"So you're turning yourself in?"

"That depends on what you and I agree to."

"Okay, Jack, I'm confused—and by the way, Heather left me and took all my money. So not only am I under suspicion of doing shit I had no knowledge of—thanks to you—I'm also broke."

"I'm sorry about your parents."

I rubbed my free hand over my eyes.

"I know they sold their stock, Buck, but at least you'll inherit—"

"Fuck you, Jack. Don't try to rationalize the situation by implying I'll be financially set, thanks to my parents' death."

When more noise sounded in the background, I recognized announcements made over a loudspeaker. Was he in an airport? Train station?

"I loved your parents, Buck. Hell, they practically raised me after mine divorced….Listen, I don't have much time here, so let me get to the point."

"Please do." Asshole.

"I want to ask you a favor."

"A *favor*? Seriously?"

"Hear me out. As I said, I told Laurie to turn evidence against me, but frankly, she's ready to do it anyway. She's going to lose everything. She'll have to move in with her parents, but she still needs money to live on."

"I can relate."

"If you can provide her a monthly stipend, I'll tell the authorities you knew nothing about what was going on at e-Antiquity, that you were too busy out in the field."

"You mean you'll tell them the truth, right?"

"You're the president of a public company, Buck. You should have known everything, and you certainly have liability. But you were so busy being the archeological rock star—" He broke off mid-sentence, though the sound of breathing on the line confirmed he was still there. "It's that simple. Help my family, and I'll confirm your ignorance."

With what money, I started to say, but realized he was banking on my inheritance.

"If you don't turn yourself in soon, they'll make me the fall guy anyway. How can I help your family then?"

"You'll figure something out, Buck. You're a smart guy."

"Not just brawn, huh?"

While I was thinking, I could hear more announcements in the background. Were they in French?

"It's a simple deal, right?" Jack's voice was distant, as if he was walking quickly, out of breath. Rushing to catch a flight, or a train?

"I'll think about it."

"Okay, I understand. This phone's a burner, so don't bother calling me back. I'll get back in touch with you in a few days."

I stuck my free hand in the water pouring down from my shower and used it to wipe my face.

"A few days may be too long, Jack."

A click sounded, then the phone went dead.

SECTION 5

5

WHEN THE MUSIC'S OVER, TURN OUT THE LIGHTS

46

THE LAW OFFICES OF STREETER, MARTIN, AND GROOMS WERE high end for a smaller firm. Dark wood trim, plush carpet, ornate Caribbean maps on the walls that appeared at least five hundred years old, though still pristine and full of brilliant color. The corridors were thick with interns and rookie attorneys fresh out of law school, all grateful to work eighty-plus hours a week in the hope that one of the partners would remember their names.

For more than forty years SMG had occupied space in the Willard Office Building on Pennsylvania Avenue, a block from the White House, and they'd fended off several merger attempts, preferring to stay small, at approximately seventy-five attorneys.

Ben and I sat in the founder's office, along with a paralegal as a witness and note taker. Carlton Grooms, Esq., was maybe five-nine, thin, approximately seventy years old, and had been our father's attorney for as long as either of us could remember. He'd been to our family farm in Middleburg for equestrian events, to both our high-school and college graduations, and now was hunched over an open folder on his desk, the corners of his lips drawn so far down they nearly reached the edges of his chin. His pallor matched the gray of his suit, but a cerulean-blue tie blazed against his starched white shirt.

When he shifted slightly in his chair, the sound of a fart broke the church-like quiet. Ben and I kept immobile, though when we were younger we'd have been biting our lips to contain hysteria. The paralegal stared straight ahead like a zombie, but it was Thursday afternoon, and she'd probably already worked a week and a half, as the clock goes.

"Your parents updated their Last Will and Testaments in May of 2006, more than two years ago." His gaze was fixed on the paper, his eyes behind narrow, heavily smudged reading glasses. "The timing may have impacted their decisions here, given the content, but, well, there's really nothing else to say about it." He glanced up at us briefly.

What was that supposed to mean? The tic in my eyelid was back.

"Terrible shame about your parents. Fine people. Dear friends." He turned his attention back to the folder and cleared his throat. The paralegal sat ready, pen in hand with a blank sheet atop her yellow notepad. Her eyes remained distant. Mr. Grooms flipped a page and read the text to himself, then flipped the next page and the next page, cleared his throat again, shook his head, and returned to the opening section.

"Their wills are mirror images…Charles and Betty Reilly, being of sound mind and body, blah, blah, blah." His eyes peered above the reading glasses as if to gauge our response when he cut to the chase.

Ben sat forward, and I reluctantly did the same. Our parents' estate had to be worth around ten million dollars, including five million from the e-Antiquity stock they'd recently dumped, though the SEC would seize it if they could connect the sale to a warning from me. The farm was owned free and clear, which at Middleburg pricing would be worth around four to five million. All their assets were held in trust to minimize estate tax, which, ironically, would now be important, but I'd gladly have traded whatever was in store to have them back.

"The wills go on, gentlemen, to describe each of your parents' trusts, both of which have the same, ah, distribution of assets. I won't bother reading every word, but I will have Emily here provide you with copies."

At mention of her name Emily flinched and lifted her pen above the page, hand quivering. She looked like she hadn't slept in weeks.

Grooms continued. "As for the personal possessions, i.e., the contents of the house, those items will be split on a fifty-fifty basis, between each of the remaining heirs and their spouses, as the case may be—"

I grunted.

Grooms glanced over his glasses, cleared his throat, and went on.

"The two of you will meet on the premises and take turns picking items until everything is accounted for. Should anything remain that none of the surviving heirs desires to have, the balance shall be donated to the Loudoun County Abused Women's Shelter."

He paused, slid both hands up under his glasses, and rubbed his eyes.

"As for the house and all liquid assets, stocks, equities, bonds, money market funds, IRAs, or other financial instruments, one hundred percent of the aggregate shall be left to Benjamin Reilly, in entirety."

The only sound that followed was the attorney's phlegmy wheeze.

"What did you say?" I said.

"Huh?" Ben suddenly sat back in his chair.

"I said that the house and one hundred percent of the liquid or invested assets go to Ben." He closed the folder softly and pulled off his glasses.

"How can that—I mean—it's not like they didn't love me—"

"Quite the contrary, Buck. They were very proud of you, but at the time that this was drawn up, you purportedly had a net worth of more than ten million dollars."

My throat felt like an inflated pufferfish—it was difficult to breathe. When I yanked my tie down to claw at my collar, my top shirt button shot off and skidded across Mr. Grooms' desk.

"I mentioned the timing, because when these wills were executed, Ben here was a recent college graduate and had nothing but school debt. Your father distinctly said—and I mean no disrespect to you, Ben—but he said that Ben was not particularly entrepreneurial and would not likely replicate Buck's success in business, so they decided to leave all their cash and the house to him."

Dead silence stretched out for at least a minute, maybe two.

"But I'm broke, guys," I said finally. "Surely we can modify that, can't we?" I turned to Ben, who'd crossed his arms and stared at Mr. Grooms. "Ben?"

"I didn't write the wills."

"But I made them most of that money!"

My brother slid sideways in his chair to face me.

"And you squandered your company, by trusting that asshole Dodson and cooking the books—"

"I was overseas! I never even looked at the books!"

"Then you're a fool."

"Boys, boys!" Mr. Grooms intervened. "Come now. I'm sure this is a shock, but the documents are signed, witnessed, and notarized. I'm sure if they'd known what was to become of your company, and, ah, marriage, Buck, they'd have changed it, but there's nothing legally we can do now."

The call Jack had made to me, proposing that I take care of his wife and kids—in exchange for his telling the truth—would only be possible if I had the money to do so.

"Ben gets it all? Are you freaking kidding me?"

Ben came right back. "Are *you* kidding *me*? What about Interpol and the FBI?"

The paralegal had come to life and was writing everything down.

"That's bullshit. I can't believe you think I had something to do with this. I did warn Dad to sell—" My head swiveled to face Mr. Grooms. "Are we under attorney-client privilege here?"

"Well, yes, technically."

"I told Dad to—"

Ben held his hands up quickly. "Don't say anything I may have to repeat in court if called to testify."

"Oh, for God's sake."

My brother wouldn't meet my stare, even though I hoped my eyes were like laser beams burning holes through his head. A thick moment of silence passed, and then another.

Finally Ben let out a huge breath.

"I won't let you starve, Buck, but like Dad said, you're entrepreneurial and I'm not. In fact, I'm bombing law school. You're not even thirty years old yet. You'll reinvent yourself, I'm sure." Suddenly he got to his feet.

Mr. Grooms stood as well. "Ben, your copies of the documents are at the front desk. Emily, please escort Mr. Reilly out and give them to him."

She jumped up and flashed Ben—the new millionaire—a coquettish smile. Bitch.

Grooms sat back heavily, making his ancient leather chair squeak. It squeaked again as he swiveled to his right, popped open a credenza, leaned over, and came up holding a bottle of single-malt Scotch and two glasses.

"No ice, I'm afraid."

"Don't need it."

I pounded the two fingers he set in front of me, and after he refilled the glass I drained that in one gulp too.

"I'm very sorry, Buck. I'll help you any way I can."

"Do you have any good defense attorneys?"

"The best. If necessary, Patrick Imperato, our top man, will handle your case."

"There's no case at all, here or in Geneva," I said. "But having the best can't hurt."

The way things had been going it might not matter what kind of case they had.

47

30 DAYS LATER

The FBI refused to meet us at SMG's offices, demanding instead that we come to the Hoover Building. Weary of seeing reporters, I hustled our group into a side entrance and was greeted by a waiting agent who took us back to the main lobby to pass through the magnetometer. Grooms, Patrick Imperato, and Jay Updegrove, my accountant, all filed into the elevator with me, then up to a conference room with Special Agent Frazier at the head of a large table, flanked by Dennis Johnson of the SEC and a man I'd never seen before. At least we weren't back in the interrogation room where I'd been interviewed before.

My team introduced themselves first, and the three government men nodded politely but maintained serious countenances throughout. The one I'd never met had a few days' growth of whiskers, something I'd thought the Bureau didn't allow.

Johnson from the SEC stated his name.

"This is François Brilland from Interpol," Frazier said.

Brilland nodded and turned to me. "I'm here on behalf of the Canton Police of Geneva, Switzerland, where your parents were killed by an automobile as they crossed Avenue de la Paix."

"Have Interpol or the police in Geneva found the car or the driver?"

"I'm here to interview *you*, Monsieur Reilly. I'll ask the questions."

"Then go ahead."

"Hang on, Buck," Grooms said. "Gentlemen, we requested this meeting to update you on matters pertaining to Mr. Reilly, and to discuss his cooperation with your investigations. However, as noted, we do have one stipulation before agreeing to—"

Frazier interrupted. "Let me stop you there, counselor. With respect to the death of his parents, we can't offer immunity to Mr. Reilly. This is an international case, and neither the FBI nor Interpol can speak on behalf of the Canton of Geneva Police."

A hard stare at me from Patrick Imperato, my defense attorney, was clearly a message of restraint. Screw that.

"Everyone knows I was virtually cut out of my parents' wills, so why would I have killed them? Makes no sense."

"But you didn't know that at the time," Frazier said. "You could have seen it as the fastest way to replenish your bank account."

"That's ludicrous!"

Brilland put in, "And we have reason to believe you were in Geneva."

"Check my passport—"

Frazier cut me off again. "When you disappeared and claimed to go fishing."

I clamped my mouth shut. I should just have revealed the money I'd buried in Maine, but it was all I had left. Would they think it incriminated me further? Fraudulent conveyance of assets?

Patrick Imperato laid a firm hand on my forearm.

"What about immunity for Mr. Reilly in any wrongdoing associated with e-Antiquity?"

Frazier turned steely eyes toward the attorney. "A wide array of charges is being considered against Mr. Reilly, just like those filed against Jack Dodson."

Would Jack really absolve me? Could he, in fact? I hadn't heard from him since that one call, and my gut told me to hedge my bets. No news about Laurie Dodson either, so I had no idea whether she was actually helping the Feds.

"The list includes falsification of financial information, self-dealing by corporate insiders, fraud, insider trading, and obstruction of justice designed to conceal criminal conduct." The agent looked from face to face. "These are very serious crimes, gentlemen, and unless you have specific evidence against Jack Dodson or know of his whereabouts, then there's zero potential for immunity for Mr. Reilly."

I sank a few inches lower in my chair.

The only sounds I could hear were my breathing and the hum of the building's air-conditioning.

"Very well," Imperato said, "we'll table the immunity discussion for now. Just know that Mr. Reilly's willing to cooperate and will do so at the appropriate time. Now, I asked Mr. Updegrove, who is Mr. Reilly's certified public accountant, to join us so he can talk about our client's bankruptcy and your allegations that—

Frazier was relentless. "Chapter Thirteen, we know. Not even gonna try and work it out, huh, Reilly?"

Brilland hadn't spoken for a while. "Bankruptcy has no bearing on the potential criminal case in Switzerland, of course."

"Nor the potential criminal charges here," Frazier said. "And, as we've stated previously, we're confident that the veil of bankruptcy could be pierced in this case, given the timing and circumstances—"

Updegrove said, "How do you figure that?"

Frazier gave him a cold glance. "We'll make our case in front of the judge, Mr. Updegrove. The fact is that if we do file charges, it will be because we're confident we have sufficient evidence against Mr. Reilly for a conviction. And, Mr. Brilland here, on behalf of the Swiss, can continue their efforts to build a case in the deaths of Mr. and Mrs. Reilly.

"So, if you have nothing further to share—such as proof of Mr. Reilly's whereabouts during those few days after his parents were killed when he disappeared, then I'm not sure why we're here."

"I was at my family's camp in Maine, dammit."

After I'd blurted out the words everyone stared at me for a long moment.

"Any witnesses to support that, Reilly?" My explanation had never satisfied Frazier. "No credit-card receipts, no toll charges on your Porsche's FastPass, no eyewitnesses that we're aware of to support that. Zip, in fact."

Brilland nodded, hard, watching me closely.

"One thing I *can* tell you."

When I sat forward, Imperato put his hand in front of my chest just like my mother would do when I was a child in her front seat and she braked suddenly.

I spoke anyway. "Jack called me, recently, and I could hear amplified announcements in the background."

"Buck, wait," Imperato said.

"Go ahead, give me something, Reilly," Frazier said. "It may help your situation."

"He called to apologize about screwing me and to offer condolences about my parents."

"When?"

"A few weeks ago, I'm not sure—"

Now it was Imperato who sat forward. "Do we have a deal on immunity?"

Frazier's eyes were on me. "Was there something you heard in the announcements?"

"Buck, please, not another word!" Imperato said.

"I'm innocent, dammit—"

Imperato slapped a hand on the table. "Not until you get a deal on immunity!"

"I'm sorry, Mr. Imperato, but I'm sick of this cat-and-mouse crap. I want them to catch him—*and* catch my parents' killers!"

"Buck, wait!" Imperato reached for me.

I went on anyway. "I'm pretty sure the announcements were in French."

Frazier nodded.

Brilland sat back. "I'll put out an alert in France."

Grooms cleared his throat. "Remember that Mr. Reilly's been cooperative, if this leads to an arrest."

The next several months were filled with depositions, interrogations, accusations, and threats from the FBI, the SEC, and Interpol on behalf of the Canton of Geneva Police Department, along with attorneys representing my darling ex-wife, Heather Drake.

These had been the worst days, weeks, months of my life.

Jack's betrayal made me finally realize I'd been a fool to trust him, regardless of our long history. I'd never heard from Jack again, and I assumed he'd decided to try his luck on the lam rather than cut a deal.

As for me, in the original maps and clues to future treasures, I'd absconded with the most valuable assets e-Antiquity had left, so I too was guilty of spiriting away corporate assets. And yes, my parents were in Switzerland on my behalf, but it hadn't been me who ran them over. Brilland could stomp around all he wanted, but there would never be a shred of evidence against me in that respect.

Brother Ben had remained distant, and even though he'd provided me with some money, I'd practically had to grovel to get it. More than once I thought of returning to the camp in Maine to retrieve my little stash, or the handgun, or even sitting inside the car, in the garage, with the engine running and the door closed.

The one thing that kept me from falling entirely into the abyss of despair was the picture of Shark Beach. I hadn't paid the mortgage in months, but since the house still hadn't sold, my plan was to squat there until dragged away by the Feds or the bank.

Was I innocent?

Nobody's entirely innocent.

Was I a monster?

I didn't think so, but a lot of people, clients, investors, academic institutions, and collectors who had lent me clues for treasures from their private collections—ones I now had copies of—had been screwed and were calling for my scalp. Lawsuits had been threatened. The attacks on television and social media were relentless. I'd become a hermit, talking only with my defense team and surviving on drive-through and delivery junk food.

Like the threatened federal cases that had yet to attain critical mass, the civil ones revved their engines but hadn't burned any rubber, yet. The reality was that I had nothing left for anyone to take.

And then one day I found two messages on my machine—I no longer answered the phone. The first one nearly knocked me to the floor.

"Monsieur Reilly, I'm calling to let you know the quid pro quo an old friend of yours offered a few months ago will soon be perfected. I cannot say more, other than advise you to keep an eye on the news, and remember to take care of the family."

Someone calling on Jack's behalf? But I was broke—I couldn't' possibly do what he'd asked me.

After the machine's beep the next surprise set me back in my chair.

"Dear Buck, I'm hoping you'll do me the honor of joining me for dinner at my club on Thursday night." I recognized the voice—Harry Greenbaum, who'd lost one of his many fortunes when the company dissolved. "Please ring back, and if so, I'll have Percy pick you up at seven. Cheers."

What would e-Antiquity's largest investor want with me?

48

FOUNDED IN 1863 WITH QUARTERS ON H STREET IN NORTHWEST D.C., the Metropolitan was one of Washington's oldest and most exclusive clubs. I'd read that virtually every president since the Civil War had been a member, and while few things intimidated me, arriving there as a failed businessman and staple of snarky TV news commentators was uncomfortable, to say the least. Even though I'd donned one of my best suits for the first time in nearly a year, I still entered the building on shaky legs.

Just inside the door was a uniformed guard, and behind the marble reception counter a sharp-eyed man scrutinized me.

"Can I help you, sir?"

"I'm here as Harry Greenbaum's guest."

The man nodded. "A porter will be right out, Mr. Reilly." In no time a tall man in a tailored blue suit escorted me through two sets of doors into a series of dark, cozy rooms, each one richly paneled in wood with thick columns of polished gray-and-white marble and clusters of tall-backed, burgundy, leather wing chairs. Smoke rose above a few of the chairs, though they were angled to make seeing their occupants impossible. My Ferragamo loafers sank into the dark plush carpet, and we glided through two more rooms until I was led to a pair of chairs with a table set between them. Harry was there, rolling white wine around in a glass.

"Ah, Buck, welcome," he said.

My guide vanished back into the darkly lit space.

Harry stood, grasped my hand, and pulled me close for an embrace.

"I'm terribly sorry for the loss of your parents. Truly awful, my dear boy."

My throat swelled, and when I tried to respond only a croak came out. I cleared my throat and tried again.

"Thank you, Harry."

"Your mother was a wonderful woman, and your father, well, America has lost one of its best statesmen."

I stood still as my host lowered his plus-size body back into the soft leather chair.

"Did you know my parents, Harry? I can't recall your meeting them at one of our investor events."

"I've known them all your life, Buck."

"They never said anything. How did you know them?"

His eyes seemed to mist for a moment and he took a long sip of wine.

"A long story for another time, dear boy."

My mind was still spinning at this revelation. My parents had never mentioned Harry, or vice versa. My whole life?

"But Jack Dodson persuaded you to back us at e-Antiquity, right?"

"Of course."

I gripped the arms of my chair tight as a waiter poured some of the white wine into my glass. My host's eyes revealed no curiosity, no hostility. When the waiter left I sucked in a breath and held it, waiting to be read the riot act, however kindly—which would just make me feel worse.

"Try the wine, Buck. It's a 1978 Châteauneuf-du-Pape. A spectacular year, and the Vieux Télégraphe is very rare."

The wine was like melted butter on my palette. "Wonderful."

Harry's gaze was steady, but his lips were slightly upturned, and I detected a softness in his eyes. After he took another sip of wine his chest sank with a long exhale.

"As for e-Antiquity," he said, "I am disappointed, of course, but it wasn't your fault. You may have erred in not being more closely involved with the rigors of public reporting, but alas, your role was in the field—and the results spoke for themselves."

My eyes brimmed for a moment. "I am sorry, Harry, for your losses and those of all our investors—"

"Part of doing business, Buck. None of us likes to lose, especially when fraud's involved, but I daresay you and Jack will suffer more than anyone."

I shook my head. "I've lost everything—and I mean *everything*."

"Years from now, when all this business is forgotten, history will always remember you as the man who found the Serpent King and proved that the Mayans indeed kept treasuries of gold and wealth, along with your many other discoveries along the way. None of that can ever be taken away from you."

I felt a brief warmth hearing his words. My back straightened, and I lifted my chin higher than it had been in ages. It wouldn't last, but it felt good.

A pair of waiters arrived, each pushing a small stainless-steel cart, and when they finished setting out the plates, a feast of seafood and roasted game hens heaped our plates, along with potatoes, wild mushrooms, and asparagus. Table leaves were opened and extended to make sure we needn't have strained from our comfortable chairs.

Once the remains of dinner were cleared a dessert wine appeared, and my heart fluttered. Surely Harry's planned agenda was about to unfold.

"The global economy is changing rapidly, Buck. Banks, financial institutions, and pillars of the last several economic cycles are tumbling like dominoes all over the world."

"Pretty ugly moment in history, for sure."

"On the contrary, dear boy. Copious opportunities abound in every country and industry. My portfolio has already jumped from twenty-four companies to thirty-two in the past six months."

Harry wasn't a shark, but he'd always had the reputation of a cagey investor with a sharp eye for upside potential—that is, leaving out e-Antiquity.

"Congratulations, then."

"The difficulty with rapid expansion, however, is ensuring proper management." He watched me, his eyes narrowed. "And knowing whom you can trust." He moistened his lips. "Which is one of the things I wanted to speak with you about."

"I'm sorry, Harry—"

"Once all is clear with e-Antiquity, I'd like to install you as the chief operating officer of one of my new companies."

What?

"Me? After the way I let Jack ruin e-Antiquity?"

"You won't allow that to happen again, and your strength is in operations, so it's a well-suited match."

I sat way back in my chair.

"A private company with strong leadership that could benefit from your acumen for field work. A combination with the potential to become world class. It would be a poetic metamorphosis for you, once all is clear, of course."

I placed my hand over my heart.

"Harry, I'm honored." I could scarcely breathe. I swallowed a couple times and cleared my throat. "I'm tempted to ask for more details, but after everything I've been through, I'm just not ready for that now—maybe ever."

He pursed his lips. "*Ever*, dear boy?"

"I'm sick of the hamster wheel. Corporate life. Ambition. Hell, marriage and relationships, for that matter." I waved a hand in the air. "I can't even look at cell phones or the Internet any more. My American dream turned out to be a nightmare."

"My father was an agricultural entrepreneur in Wales, and he taught me that life is like farming," Harry said. "Droughts one year followed by abundance another. Field rotation, letting one go fallow only to plant it with new crops the following year, led to greater production on the whole." He held up his glass. "Good therapy, too, taking time off. You've seen the world and, provided the road ahead is clear, you'll have to choose a new direction."

He leaned forward, elbows on the table, with a gleam in his eye. "So, what will you do for an encore?"

"You mean after I'm finished being scathed by the Feds?"

"Assuming that works out, where will you go?"

"I have an idea—a place we visited during my childhood, where all my memories were happy ones. A place where I can stay off the grid, lead a quiet life, and heal my wounds."

"A resort town? On the water?"

My eyes narrowed. "Yeah, that's right."

"I have investments and board positions with two major hospitality firms," Harry said. "Between them, they have more than five thousand keys, or rooms, if you will, in some wonderful locations. Perhaps I can be of assistance."

"Well, I'm planning to check out for a while—a long while—as soon as possible."

Harry nodded. "Jack will be doing the same thing, albeit from prison." The message on my answering machine alluding to Jack!

Harry chuckled at my expression. "I take it you haven't seen the news."

"What happened?"

"He turned himself in outside Paris this afternoon."

I was so taken aback I couldn't speak for a minute, but Harry was patient.

"Did he have suitcases of cash—our cash?" I asked.

"Mmm, afraid not. No sign of the money he'd taken, but perhaps he'll negotiate with the authorities for a reduced sentence."

Take care of the family. Did that part of the message from the emissary mean Jack would clear me? I'd never told him that I accepted his deal, and I had no money to help, but a flicker of hope lit a pilot light in my soul.

I licked my lips. "He deserves whatever he gets. He lied to us all, Harry. I'm not sure how much he skimmed over the years, but it had to be millions."

Percy, Harry's driver, appeared next to us. "The car is out front, Mr. Greenbaum."

"Right. So, Buck, let me know where you intend to go, and if I don't own part of a hotel there, I'll know people who do." A twinkle lit in his eye, and he raised an eyebrow. "And someday, we'll figure out how you can help me recover the twenty million dollars I lost in e-Antiquity."

After that caught me off guard, my hand was like putty in his.

Once he left I sat back in the plush wingback chair and rolled the remains of the Châteauneuf-du-Pape around my glass as I'd seen Harry do. The fact that he'd known my parents for twenty-odd years was a shocker, and for the life of me I couldn't figure out why neither party had shared that with me. And his offer to install me as an executive officer at another company was equally surprising. Being in the field, thinking on my feet, searching for missing items and operating on my own had been where I'd excelled. I couldn't imagine where I'd get another such opportunity, but now wasn't the time. Not now, maybe not ever.

From the corner of my eye I noticed a man heading toward me. It was the same blue suit that had led me here initially. He stopped at my chair.

"I'll lead you out, Mr. Reilly."

I could add being escorted out of the Metropolitan Club to my long list of indignities.

49

For the next several days my house was under siege by news teams. Jack's arrest—a well-publicized corporate fugitive who surrendered after being pursued in an international manhunt—was big news. One of the more interesting exclamation points to the tsunami of corporate failures, mortgage scams, and other components of the global economic meltdown. Villains were needed to take the blame for their greedy excess, with Jack a favorite media target thanks to his disappearance and the nature of our business, and I was the ideal co-target, thanks to my fame.

Would the Feds cut me any slack since my lead about Jack proved true? Yes, he'd turned himself in, but in France, where I'd suggested they search. That had to be worth something.

Leftovers and liquor were in short supply, and if I didn't get out of the house soon I'd starve or go insane. My stockpile of cash on hand had dwindled to pocket change, aside from what was buried in Maine, and I was a squatter in my own home. Mr. Grooms was still covering my legal expenses using the contingency he'd set aside from my parents' estate. I didn't even try to reach Heather, knowing that what I was going through was of no interest to her other than its effect on her image. Apparently being on the arm of the ancient French billionaire didn't count.

Yeah. I had to get out. And I finally had a plan.

Unfortunately, my plan required significantly more capital than I had, even if the house sold in the next five minutes and I added the stash up in Maine. So for an entire afternoon I researched, took notes, wrote, and refined a speech until I sharpened an angle that had something more than a snowball in the tropics' chance to succeed.

With sunglasses on and headlights off, I started the Porsche in my garage. Nowadays I backed in to facilitate rapid escapes, and before the door was up all the way I revved it, popped the clutch—the tires chirped on the concrete—and lit out like Bruce Wayne from the Bat Cave. Newsmen jumped out of the way before they could lift their cameras as I shot out of the driveway.

"Screw you, buzzards!"

Down Georgetown Pike to Route 7, then Route 28 to Route 50 and down into Middleburg, where I blew through town headed for the family's—Ben's—farm. I downshifted and turned the Porsche hard onto Zulla Road—cut off an SUV, and accelerated up the two-lane road. A couple of miles further I turned into the driveway at speed and slid sideways in the gravel as I braked to a stop. Luckily Ben opened the front door and met me on the porch, so I didn't have to ring the bell.

"You in a hurry, big brother?"

"To get on with my life? Damn straight."

Inside everything looked the same. We settled in the kitchen, and Ben broke out a couple of Coors Light. I provided a quick rundown on the e-Antiquity situation. He was up on the news about Jack and his disclaimer on the innuendoes about my involvement. Ben mentioned nothing of the trumped-up speculation about charges from Switzerland, which I hoped was a good sign.

"Virginia must feel pretty small for you," he said.

"Based on Jack's cooperation, my attorneys say I should be free to travel. I can't disappear, but they can't hold me indefinitely without filing charges, and I certainly don't want charges filed."

He nodded, listening—exactly what I wanted. He was in the mansion, and I was in the outhouse.

"There's a purchase offer on my house for less than my mortgage, but the lender approved a short sale. I filed bankruptcy papers, so I'll be losing everything else soon. Yeah, Virginia feels small for a lot of reasons."

Ben finished his beer, went to the fridge, and took out two more. I hadn't touched mine.

From my jacket pocket I pulled out the old photograph of all of us on Shark Beach and laid it on the table. Ben's eyes followed my hand, his eyes suddenly going wide.

"I remember that day! What did we call that—Shark Key?"

"Shark Beach."

"Yeah, oh man, that was amazing." He grinned. "And Mom, look at her face, she was so pissed at Dad." When he laughed out loud, it was the first time we'd shared such a moment since our parents' death.

"We might not always have seen eye to eye, Ben, or been close, but we'll always be brothers."

He put the photo back on the table and stared at me, waiting.

"I need your help," I said.

He frowned. "With what?"

"I want to buy a seaplane."

"The hell for?"

"The next phase of my life."

He bit off the smile and narrowed his eyes. "What's this got to do with me, Buck?"

"If I can get a plane, I'm moving to Key West. Figure that's as good a place as any to reinvent myself."

"End of the world, I guess that makes sense."

I shrugged. "If I can't get a plane, though, I'll stick around here. When my house sells, I'll probably have to move in with you, if that's okay."

Ben took another slug of beer. Now I drank some too, waiting.

"Seaplane, huh? Running drugs your next big idea?"

I laughed. "Just a little charter business. Quiet, and peaceful. I'm done with corporate America. Done with chasing wealth and riches. I'm glad things worked out so you got Mom and Dad's money. Hell, the IRS would've taken my share anyway. I'm just looking to live a simple life under the radar."

"Pretty young for a last resort," Ben said.

"Last resort." I smiled. "Hm. I might just have to use that. Last Resort Charters." I thought for a second, then added, "and Salvage."

The gears in Ben's head were turning, I could see it in his eyes. He'd never been able to conceal his internal debates.

"What kind of plane were you thinking?"

I didn't smile. I pressed my lips tight and pulled an *Airplane Trader* magazine from of my back pocket to open to a dog-eared page.

"Cessna Caravan on floats is perfect for what I have in mind. Single engine, typically seats nine passengers, but I could get a waiver and seat up to fourteen—"

"How much do those run, used?"

"This one here's a 2002 with only nine hundred thirty-three hours—"

"I don't know what that means. What's it cost?"

"It's a steal at two point one million."

"Dollars? Are you crazy?" Ben's chair screeched across the floor as he stood up to pace around the kitchen.

"Plane like that will last forever—"

"I'm not spending two million dollars, Buck. No damn way." He grabbed the *Airplane Trader*. "Let me see this thing."

He flipped pages, his eyes as intense as I'd ever seen them. He stopped, read something, and held the magazine up.

"Here, how about this one?"

He'd stabbed his index finger on an ad for a Cessna 152.

"That won't work, Ben—"

"Why, not fancy enough?"

"Not enough seating or horsepower."

He grunted and flipped a few pages forward. "This one?" A Cessna 172.

"I need one with floats so I can land in the water around the Keys."

He slapped more pages around until he was near the back, where he paused. His lip curled and he pushed the magazine over up for closer inspection. I held my tongue but knew exactly what was coming.

"Okay, this costs a lot more than the Cessna 172, but a quarter of that Caravan." He dropped the magazine on the table in front of me. "And it's a classic. A Grumman Widgeon—says it was freshly restored."

I pulled the magazine closer, but having already read that listing a dozen times and spoken to the owner, I knew the details.

"A plane built back in forty-six? That's what you're suggesting?"

"Costs five hundred thousand! You're damned lucky I'd even consider that."

We held a long stare until I glanced away and let out my breath.

"So if it checks out, you'll give me the money?"

"Not exactly," he said. "Before I explain, I want you to know something. I don't believe you had anything to do with Mom and Dad's death, even if they were in Switzerland on your behalf."

A rush of emotion had me reach for my beer to gulp down a mouthful. I knew he'd never believed it, but I also knew how hard it was for him to admit it.

"I also think you're an irresponsible former playboy who sucks with money."

"What's that supposed to mean?"

"I'll *lend* you money for the plane." He took a sip of beer. "And when you get it, you're moving to Key West?"

"As soon as possible."

The smile that bent his lips was like a kick to my shin.

The Widgeon was the plane I'd wanted all along. I knew he wouldn't spring for the Cessna, and the Widgeon, I learned when I called the owner, had once belonged to Jimmy Buffett. He'd crashed it during a water take-off near Nantucket that had nearly killed him. But the plane had been restored and would be perfect for what I had in mind.

Ben and I went around the house with a pad and paper, taking turns picking out pieces of furniture, paintings, knick-knacks, and items that had sentimental meaning to us. Upstairs in the master bedroom I found Dad's old trunk under the bed. It was a footlocker where he'd kept souvenirs, mementoes, old photographs, letters, documents, and journals. It too had been forbidden territory.

My heart rate accelerated. I glanced at Ben, who was staring at the antique bed and matching dressers. Given that his clothes were in the closet, he'd already moved in here. His mental wheels were turning so hard I imagined smoke coming from his ears.

"Tell you what," I said. "You can keep all the bedroom furniture, and I'll take this old trunk full of Dad's junk."

His eyes flared for a moment. "Done."

Ben didn't have a sentimental bone in his body. Didn't make him a bad guy, it was just how he was wired. Not wanting to leave the trunk here for him to pilfer later, I got him to help me drag it down the stairs. My two bins of personal items from my house were in the Porsche, so we lugged it all to the tack room in the horse barn, now empty since he'd already sold or given away the horses.

"I'll give you the key," Ben said. "You can store all your stuff here."

Over the next hour we carried the few other articles from my parents' house that I thought I could use, once I got my feet back on the ground. Mostly art, photos, Dad's desk and chair, and more stuff from his study.

With the tack room padlocked, I took a slow walk around and then went back to the house to say goodbye to my brother. I'd be leaving for Connecticut in the morning to check out the plane.

After an awkward hug, he followed me out to my car.

I stopped halfway. "One other thing, Ben."

"What's that?"

"Jack Dodson called me a few months ago to make a deal."

Ben took a step back. "Before he got arrested? What kind of deal?"

"He promised to tell the truth and admit I had no knowledge of his fraudulent activities if we'd provide his wife and kids a monthly stipend."

"*We?* Why the hell would I—"

"Because, otherwise, the Feds could seize everything you inherited from Mom and Dad. They know that Dad sold all his e-Antiquity stock just days before we were shut down, and Jack could easily help them make a case against us."

His Adam's apple bobbed up and down. "They could seize it all?"

"In the blink of an eye."

His vacant stare was a window into his fear. I felt like saying it sucked to be rich and lose everything, but for once I held back.

"So much for Jack-off being like a member of our family." I saw the long breath he let out as another sign of capitulation.

"I'm thinking a few thousand a month," I said.

"I'll deduct it from what I was going to lend you."

He winked at me, which made me smile.

"Funny, Ben."

As the younger sibling, he'd long been in my shadow and had never enjoyed the upper hand in our relationship. That, and our emotional distance caused by my choosing Jack's company over his, had been a long, slow burn. Part of me enjoyed seeing him with responsibility now. The rest of me resented the hell out of it, but I'd play along.

"I'll call you after I see the plane. Tomorrow, okay?"

"Sure, Buck. I'll be here."

With that, I drove slowly down the long oak-lined driveway, wondering when I'd ever return.

50

THE OLD WIDGEON CHECKED OUT FINE. AFTER BEING CAPSIZED off Nantucket, the plane had been hauled to a private hangar in Connecticut, where it was restored to operable form. By no means pristine, it still had a smart new paint job of arctic white covering the fuselage and bold red stripes from the nose along the waterline to the tail. The mechanic who walked me through the logbook and took me for a test flight had closed each hatch, gently pulled every lever, and sat gingerly in each seat, his affinity for the plane obvious. What I found most interesting was that the floats below the wings were different colors—green under the port wing, red under the starboard.

"What's with the different-colored floats?" I said.

He smiled. "They're the same colors as channel markers. Green on your port side is outbound, and red on the right means you're headed toward home."

Headed toward home.

The idea comforted me and gave me an instant connection with the sixty-plus-year-old amphibian. With all my other pre-bankruptcy possessions soon to be controlled by the court, the plane would be the only thing of tangible value I'd own, thanks to Ben.

When it came time to negotiate the details, I was referred to an attorney for the owner. We haggled over the price, but given that it still belonged to the rock star, he didn't really need money but felt jinxed by the plane since he'd nearly died in it.

We agreed on price and, when I extended my hand to shake, the attorney reached for the phone instead. "Before we shake, the seller wanted to speak with you."

The attorney dialed a number and the speakerphone crackled to life.

"Is this *the* Buck Reilly?" He had a strong Southern accent. "The big shot archeologist?"

"Yes sir, that's me—or the former me, I should say."

"Damn, boy, a lot of water under the hull since I saw you on that big yacht in St. Barths."

The image of the yacht we'd rented to schmooze our investors was like a memory from a previous life. I'd remembered Buffett playing a show on the quay for Le Select.

"You might say that," I said.

"If you guys are calling me, it's because all the details are set. My question, are you going to be able to take care of Lady of the Waters? That's what I call the Widgeon."

I breathed in deeply and let it out slow.

"She'll be my only lady in the world."

Apparently my answer was sufficient, because the attorney gave the all-clear sign to continue, and the plane became mine.

It took a day for Ben's wire transfer to come in, but when I finally climbed inside the plane, alone, ducked down, and squeezed forward to sit in the left seat, I stayed there for a while just soaking up the feel of the cockpit. Far simpler than more modern planes, the Widgeon did have new electronics, but the instrument panel, most of the gauges, the seats, and the paint were stock—scratched, dinged, and threadbare—which made me feel even more at one with her.

She needed a new name. I couldn't think of her as Lady of the Waters, even though it sounded regal, and some considered changing the name of a craft bad luck. But I didn't want to attract attention, and Buffett fans would flock to see the plane if they knew it had been his.

I took my time with the pre-flight process, frequently consulting the laminated card that outlined the sequential steps.

When restored, the plane had been converted to a McKinnon Super Widgeon with twin Lycoming 295-horsepower engines. I'd already done the walk-around outside, made sure the drain plugs were firmly installed, climbed onto the wings and verified that both ninety-gallon tanks were full of 100-octane fuel. Inside, I switched the fuel selector to the port tank and adjusted the carburetor to full rich, cold, the propellers to full forward. Elevator and rudder tabs were neutral and the tail wheel was locked. I primed the throttle for the starboard engine, flipped the ignition switches to ON, and engaged the starter.

The starboard engine spun a few times—WHOOSH!—and kicked on.

The Widgeon shook, but with a solid feel. Chatter registered in my headset. Igor Sikorsky Airport in Bridgeport was good-sized and also had helicopter traffic. I keyed the mic and alerted the tower that I was prepared to take off. They directed me to taxi toward Runway 24, which was 4,677 feet long.

Oil pressure registered positive. When I repeated the same process for the port engine—WHOOSH!—it fired up, and the plane's vibration balanced out evenly.

There was no mirror where I could see myself, but I felt my mouth spread in a broad smile.

I was free.

I hadn't flown in months, had never owned my own plane, but I'd chartered everything from Piper Cubs to Gulfstream jets. Now there was no place I had to be, nobody waiting for me, no country, city, university, or museum to appease, no schedule, no team.

I'd lost everything. I'd lost the people I loved most—some had been killed, others had abandoned me. All the material trappings I'd cared about over the past several years were gone, including my house and car, all my cash and investments, everything. All I had left was a folder full of copies of old maps, letters, and clues to potential treasures around the world that e-Antiquity hadn't pursued, because it had lain in my undiscovered safe at home. My father had taken the originals with him, and I hoped he'd deposited them somewhere in Switzerland, but even they were off my mental radar. And now I had this sixty-plus-year-old flying boat, and my gas tanks were full. Adrenalin coursed through my body and into my hands.

Directed by Air Traffic Control to proceed, I increased the RPMs and hurtled forward at full throttle—the tail dragger shimmied and swayed slightly—until two-thirds of the way down the runway we hit critical speed and lifted off. Our climb speed was 120 miles per hour. At 10,000 feet we were traveling at 170 miles per hour, and ATC vectored us south.

"Our first take-off, just you and me, old girl," I said. "The first of many, I hope."

Rebirth!

"It's a fresh start… Lady." I smiled. "But if you don't mind, I'm going to change your name. Not sure to what yet, but we'll know it when it happens, right?"

I was talking to the airplane. Crazy?

Nah. The bond I'd felt with the plane, really since I first spotted it in the *Airplane Trader*, had been instant. It had grown immensely when I set my eyes on her, and after the mechanic took me on the checkout ride I knew we were right for each other. But now, alone together, above the clouds, with nothing but the future on our horizon, the warmth of trust, caring, and comfort permeated my body and soul.

"I promise to take care of you, old girl." I glanced around the inside of the cockpit and checked all the flight indicators, which held solid. "Please do the same for me."

51

I RENTED A CAR AT LEESBURG AIRPORT AND HEADED SOUTH. I'D promised Grooms that I'd call him once back in Virginia, but when I powered on my cell phone I saw dozens of missed calls. Out of curiosity, I scrolled through them. One number jumped out repeatedly: Special Agent Frazier of the FBI.

"Frazier here."

I took my foot off the gas pedal of the econobox and coasted down Route 15.

"I'm leaving Virginia, Frazier. Going to a place where the climate matches my state of mind."

A couple beats passed. "We can't hold you, but don't fall off the face of the earth. You know we'll find you when we need to."

A smile tugged at my lips. "My attorney will know where to reach me."

I hit End.

I had one last call to make before ending this chapter of my life.

"Harry Greenbaum."

"It's Buck Reilly. Just calling to let you know I'm leaving today."

"Wonderful, dear boy. Where have you decided to go?"

"Key West. Not sure for how long, but I have a lot of special memories there."

"Ah, yes. The family vacations you mentioned, no doubt."

"Right."

"As fate would have it, one of my hospitality companies owns the La Concha Hotel there. I'll make arrangements on your behalf. Stay as long as you'd like."

Tears suddenly filled my eyes.

"Thank you, Harry."

"Do keep in touch, Buck."

Once I arrived at the farm in Middleburg, I found a note on the front door.

Buck,

Sorry I'm not here to say goodbye. I put your gear in the barn next to the tack room. You padlocked the door, so I couldn't get in. With everything going on, it's kind of hard to say goodbye. I hope you'll understand.

I'll send you a check for $10,000 every month to cover your expenses until you get your feet back on the ground. I hope the new plane will help you launch your charter business. Let me know what your address and phone number is when you get settled.

Take care, Ben."

I brushed a tear off my cheek.

The sun was high in the clear blue sky as I walked around the back of the house, down the gravel path through Mom's garden, already overgrown with weeds. I hoped Ben would hire a gardener. Past the garden was the worn path to the barn, where I stopped to slowly turn in a circle to take in the family property one last time. The fall foliage painted a dazzling palette.

With a knot in my throat, I found my duffel bags of clothes and possessions on the concrete floor outside the tack room, with an envelope on top. Inside were a hundred $100 bills—my first installment of Ben's allowance. On a good day at the height of e-Antiquity, I'd averaged that much an hour.

Inside the tack room, I sat in the chair from Dad's office and stared at the old metal army trunk. I was tempted to root through it, but the loss of my parents was still too raw to handle the mementoes and trinkets he'd felt strongly enough about to keep. His words from the last time I'd seen him—about not always having been a Boy Scout and living below the radar himself—made me wonder if there were any hints of that life in here.

"Someday, Dad."

I relocked the tack room, walked straight to my rental car without looking around the property again, and returned to Leesburg Regional Airport. With my gear stowed aboard the plane, I paid cash to have the fuel tanks replenished, then did the pre-flight check.

"Well, old girl, this is everything now, aside from what I left at the farm." I spoke as I went through the checklist inside the plane. "You might find this hard to believe, but a year ago I was on top of the world. But as you know from your… incident off Nantucket, things can change quickly.

And my mom taught me that what matters most is how you respond to adversity."

I glanced out the port window to check the flaps as I pressed my foot down on the left pedal, then glanced to starboard as I checked the right.

"We're quitting the rat race, you and me." I took the folder of copied treasure maps from the backpack and placed them in the small locker under my seat in the cockpit. "But I'll keep these in case we ever change our minds."

There was no air traffic control at Leesburg, so I cranked up the engines, announced my intentions to traffic in the flight pattern, and taxied to the head of the runway. As I started down the mile of asphalt, I couldn't see what waited at the other end, but knowing intuitively that it would be okay, I pressed the throttles forward and began the next phase of my uncharted journey.

52

It took one long day to get there, but as the mainland disappeared, I glanced down to see the water of Florida Bay.

"You see that clear mint-green water?" I said. "That's what you'll be landing in from now on. No more brown or murky waters for us."

A thin line of surf separated the green water from the mustard flats. That's where my life was now. In the turbulence of the surf, pounding against the shore.

We continued on a southwest heading, and for the thirty minutes it took to reach Key West I was able to watch the narrow strips of land that made up the Florida Keys. Miami Control vectored me around commercial traffic and the south end of the island.

I hadn't cut my hair for going on three months. My new moustache now looked as if I'd had it for years, so there was little resemblance to my former slick Wall Street appearance. One of the things that I loved about Key West was that people didn't pry. All its residents were welcome to live their lives in peace as one human family.

"What d'you think about Last Resort Charter and Salvage?"

The plane flew steadily, so I took that as a positive.

"Permission to land, Grumman N1475," Miami Control said.

We entered base leg right over the western end of Duval Street, the silver roofs of resort hotels and century-old Conch homes reflecting the bright sunlight of the afternoon. We descended onto Runway 09 as palm trees and brilliant blue water shot past my starboard window. We only needed half of the 4,801-foot runway to slow sufficiently, and I exited onto the taxiway toward the fixed base operation and general aviation terminal where I found an empty spot on the ramp to tie down.

Once the engines were shut down, the batteries off, and quiet filled the cockpit, I leaned back and let out a long breath.

"We're home, old girl."

With my backpack over my shoulder, I hunched down and made my way to the hatch, popping it open to find a man standing outside the plane. He was average height, had a chunky physique, was wearing a red Hawaiian shirt, and rubbing his grease-stained hands on a heavily stained rag. I heard him whistle as I climbed outside.

"Got yourself an old beauty there," he said.

"She needs a little work, but yeah, thanks."

He shuffled from his left foot to his right foot for an awkward moment, then tentatively held out his hand.

"I'm Ray Floyd, chief mechanic here."

"Buck Reilly."

When he looked me over, I couldn't tell if he recognized my name or was just shy.

"You planning to stay here long?"

"Not sure, but I hope so." I smiled. "For now I'm taking a little vacation, but we'll see what happens."

"Careful, Key West is where vacations become permanent. I'd be real happy to help you if she, ah, needs anything. What's her name?"

I looked back at the Widgeon. The horizon behind her had taken on an orange glow as sunset approached. My mother's face popped into my head, for she would always rush outside at dusk to see the sunset.

"Betty," I said. "Her name's Betty."

Ray Floyd nodded and glanced from Betty to me, then smiled.

"Welcome to Key West, Buck and Betty."

Epilogue

HAPPY HOUR ON THE SOUTHERNMOST BEACH WAS A FINE WAY TO spend an afternoon. It hadn't taken me long to settle into the slow pace of island life, and even though there was a lot of traffic into and out of Key West, I managed to get numb to it after a couple weeks. Ben had shipped my father's 1966 Land Rover Series A 88 from the farm in Middleburg down on a flatbed trailer. He'd said it was a gift, but I suspected he didn't want the scraped-up old classic littering his backyard.

"Another beer, Buck?"

I flipped the wooden Happy Hour token to Fletcher, the proprietor.

"Thanks."

I sat facing the creamy green water while I listened to another Virginian, Dave McKenney, covering Buffett tunes interspersed with original music. The chorus to a song he said had been inspired in Key West had me smiling and nodding along.

"Cuz I got me a long view
Off a very short pier.
I got plenty to do,
But I'm-a sitting right here,

Staring out across the water,
Past bikinis a-getting hotter,
It's a day worth of drinking,
And my mind ain't thinking too clear…"

Fletcher brought me a cold beer. "This shit'll kill you," he said.

"Nobody would notice."

"You're not paying attention." He nodded toward a pair of attractive ladies in bikinis smiling openly at me.

"That'll kill you faster," I said.

Fletcher laughed and walked off.

My hair had grown even longer, my moustache bushier, and I couldn't really remember what an Armani suit looked like. There were only three things I wanted now: a beauty to rescue, a battle to fight, and maybe, someday, a treasure to find.

Dave's lyrics again made me smile

"Gonna live an island thriller,
Full of treasure, rum and killers,
Throw in some romance,
And a fistfight, or two…"

I held my half-full beer up toward the horizon. "Cheers to that."

About the Author

John H. Cunningham is the author of the best selling, six book, Buck Reilly adventure series, which includes Red Right Return, Green to Go, Crystal Blue, Second Chance Gold, Maroon Rising and Free Fall to Black. Through the years, John has been a bouncer at a Key West nightclub, a diver, pilot, magazine editor, commercial developer, song writer and global traveler. He has either lived in or visited the many island locations that populate the series, and has experienced or witnessed enough craziness and wild times to keep the Buck Reilly series flowing. John mixes fact with fiction and often includes real people in his novels, like Jimmy Buffett, Chris Blackwell, Matt Hoggatt, Thom Shepherd, Dave McKenney and Bankie Banx to augment the reader's experience. Adhering to the old maxim, "write what you know," John's books have an authenticity and immediacy that have earned a loyal following and strong reviews.

John lives in Virginia and Key West, and spends much of his time traveling. His choices for the places and plots that populate the Buck Reilly series include many subjects that he loves: Key West, Cuba, Jamaica, and multiple Caribbean settings, along with amphibious aircraft, colorful characters, and stories that concern themselves with the same tensions and issues that affect all of our lives.

Long View Off a Short Pier
Dave McKenney and John H. Cunningham

I'm a lover and a writer,
Mental heavyweight fighter
Slingin words on a page
Like a silver tongue devil with a keyboard for a blade
Trying to save women while my deadline is chillin'
Throwing down stories one word at a time

Got another novel done
Time to sit out in the sun
Gonna plan my escape
Maybe get my ass south to the Keys or the Cape
I'm Headed to the water where there's no-one I can bother
No place that I need to be, and I just don't care

Cuz I got me a long view
Off a very short pier
I got plenty to do
But I'm-a sitting right here
Staring out across the water
Past bikinis a-getting hotter
It's a day worth of drinking and my mind ain't thinking too clear

Morning starts with Cuban coffee
And the air is smelling salty
I can hear the ocean call
But my agent is-a screamin'
And I'm telling him to stall
Gonna write an Island thriller full of treasure, rum and killers
Throw in some romance and a fistfight or two

Cuz I got me a long view
Off a very short pier
I got plenty to do,
But I'm-a sitting right here
Staring out across the water
Past bikinis a-getting hotter
It's a day worth of drinking and my mind ain't thinking too clear

I am a lover and a writer,
A literary prize fighter
Stabbing words on the page
Like a silver tongue devil with a keyboard for a blade
Turning real life into fiction,
Set to music is my mission,
Write a hit song with a badass musician, or two

Cuz I got me a long view
Off a very short pier
I got plenty to do
But I'm-a sitting right here
Staring out across the water
Past bikinis a-getting hotter
It's a day worth of drinking and my mind ain't thinking too clear
It's a day worth of drinking and my mind ain't thinking too clear

For John's other books and music, you can go to his website and link from there: www.jhcunningham.com

Book links:

RED RIGHT RETURN (Buck Reilly book 1):
www.amazon.com/Right-Return-Reilly-Adventure-Series-ebook/dp/B00D8HOSN2/

GREEN TO GO (Buck Reilly book 2):
www.amazon.com/Green-Buck-Reilly-Adventure-Series-ebook/dp/B00D6Q0WOE/

CRYSTAL BLUE (Buck Reilly book 3):
www.amazon.com/Crystal-Blue-Reilly-Adventure-Series-ebook/dp/B00EWSAZ92/

SECOND CHANCE GOLD (Buck Reilly book 4):
www.amazon.com/Second-Chance-Reilly-Adventure-Series/dp/0985442271/

MAROON RISING (Buck Reilly book 5):
www.amazon.com/Maroon-Rising-Buck-Reilly-Adventure-ebook/dp/B016QUC76C

Music links:

"THE BALLAD OF BUCK REILLY" (Download the song or all of Workaholic in Recovery from iTunes at):
https://itunes.apple.com/us/album/workaholic-in-recovery/id908713680

"RUM PUNCH" by Thom Shepherd, and co-written by John H. Cunningham, is available on iTunes at:
https://itunes.apple.com/us/album/rum-punch-single/id1051324975

"LONG VIEW OFF A SHORT PIER" by Dave McKenney and co-written by John H. Cunningham, is available on iTunes at:
https://itunes.apple.com/us/album/back-in-time/id1161935367

CPSIA information can be obtained
at www.ICGtesting.com
Printed in the USA
FSOW01n2023210417
33430FS